Witch Moon

JACK LAFOUNTAIN

House of Honor Books

House of Honor

The characters and events portrayed in this book are fictitious. Any similarity to real persons, living or dead, is coincidental and not intended by the author.

ISBN: 978-1-68596-085-8

Printed in the United States of America

Published by House of Honor Books.

Harvest, Alabama

DEDICATION

This book is dedicated to my daughter, Darline who during the writing of this book, demonstrated for me that good things can be captured if pursued long enough.

PROLOGUE

Paul Poulard stared across his desk hoping the woman seated there could not see the desperation in his eyes. He knew in his heart the attempt to appear calm was failing badly. He could read it in her smug smile. He unfolded his hands, and placed them flat on his desk, before, a moment later, refolding them in front of himself. What she was proposing was monstrous. Thoughts of the deed had crossed his mind in moments of depression. They were quickly brushed aside as the sin they were. The woman had pushed it beyond temptation into a screaming compulsion. His racing mind was a runaway train that could not be stopped.

She opened her purse, placed the gun on his desk and gently slid it toward him. Her smile widened enough for him to see her sharp white teeth. She wanted him to do it, hungered for him to do it while she watched. He could see it in her eyes.

"Of course, the choice is yours, Father," her silken voice told him. "Whichever you choose, you will be leaving the church before the sun comes up tomorrow. I have my preference, but the choice is yours. Free will, that's how this business of yours work, isn't it?"

"Why are you doing this?" Father Poulard asked, unable to keep his voice from quaking.

"You know why. You're wasting time," she said. "But it's your time to waste. I will leave you to it. There's not much left."

She rose from her chair, gave him a fresh flicker of a smile and a slight bow of her head. She glided to the door in graceful easy steps whose allure was lost on the terrified man. She paused, door partially open, to look over her shoulder at him.

"Sleep well, Father," she said and began to laugh.

In his youth Father Paul had friends blown apart

beside him and heard the cries of those not lucky enough to die immediately. He still heard them in his dreams. Yet, the sound of her mirth at his plight sent a chill through him unlike any sound he'd ever heard. He stared down at the gun in front of him. Sweat beaded in his forehead as he fought a yo-yo battle of wills with his right hand. Each time it crept toward the weapon the tattered remains of his mind pulled it back.

It's a mortal sin, he reminded himself. *It's blasphemy. But how is that worse than the other choice? God help me.*

He laid his forehead on his arms crossed on the desk in front of him. He wasn't a weak man, but heart frozen with fear, he wept until a voice whispered his name. He didn't look up, unsure that he really heard a voice at all. It came again accompanied by a faint stirring of the air. It was the feeling of being watched that finally coaxed his head up. The room seemed empty, but he knew it wasn't.

"Show yourself," he demanded, but there was no strength in his words.

His hand went to the crucifix about his neck and nervously turned it over repeatedly.

"In the name of Christ—"

"Stop right there," a voice from across the room interrupted him.

The bookshelf behind him seemed to be dissolving in front of his eyes. It took him a moment to realize the shelf wasn't melting away. A mist hung in the air between him and the books he loved. The near transparent fog swirled in on itself as it coalesced into the shape of a woman. She was no more solid than the cloud. Without legs below the knees, she floated above the floor. Her pale spectral form bobbed on a breeze Paul could not feel. Slowly, almost reluctantly, a beautiful face emerged.

Is this an angel?

He wasn't sure and picked the gun up with quaking hands. He held the pistol out of sight between his knees, barrel aimed at the floor, and waited to see what would happen. When she did not react to the weapon, he spoke to her.

"Who are you—what are you? Tell me."

"I am your salvation"' came a voice more solid and real than the mouth which spoke to him.

"You're not an angel. I know you."

"I am a figment of the world's imagination."

"I...I don't...I don't understand," the priest stammered. "I've seen you in this church. You're...uh...you're...Stephanie Cross.

"Of course, you don't understand," she replied with a titter of laughter. "Nothing to get hung up about. I don't exist, everyone says so. That's the beauty of it. I can tell the truth, and no one believes it—not anymore. Hathorne knew, but he's long dead and I'm just the long dead superstition that put an end to him."

"I knew it. The evidence was always real, wasn't it?"

"Of course, why do you think they want you dead? But it's not just dead, is it? They want more."

"You're with them. So, why are you here? How could you possibly be my salvation?"

"With them? No, but like them. That is, the one using my specter is like them. I'm quite innocent."

"Then it's...it's—"

"True? Don't you believe your own writing?' she asked. "But enough of that. The one who just left here means to see you, not just dead, but consigned to hell, am I correct?"

"Yes."

"And, of course, you would rather not go. I am here to offer you a third choice," she said. "One, shall we say, only a tiny bit less hopeless."

He lifted his crucifix and held it in her direction.

"Be gone."

"Very well, but not because of that cross. Hand it to me if you don't believe me," she replied holding out a ghostly hand. "No? Then I will leave you to choose which of the other paths you will take.'

She drifted toward the shelves dissolving back into a mist as she went.

"No, wait," he urged. "I will hear what you have to say. You're not Stephanie. Tell me who and what you are."

"You are, of course, familiar with, Hebrews 11:1?" she asked.

"Yes."

"Well, let's hear it," she prodded, voice rife with impatience.

"Now faith is the substance of things hoped for, the evidence of things not seen," he quoted.

"Very good," she replied with a silent clap of her less than solid hands. "About three hundred years ago, I was the unseen evidence that sent the innocent to the gallows and set the guilty free."

"What's that supposed to mean?"

"You figure it out," she snapped. "Meanwhile, if you wish to save yourself go to Lockett, Louisiana, and find a man named Landry. If I were you, I'd hurry. Your visitor will be back for you before dawn."

The woman returned to mist and, on a gust of wind that came from within the closed room, blew through the books.

Paul, breathing through his open mouth, dropped into his chair. He laced his white-knuckled fingers through one another to keep them from shaking. The quaking merely migrated up his arms and over his body. After some minutes, the tremors stopped, and the rush of his thoughts began. He wrestled with himself though the outcome was never in question.

What do I have to lose that is not already lost?

Tucking the gun into his pocket, he walked out of

his office and through the church doors. He stepped out onto the wide steps to look up and down the street. On an adjacent corner a man leaned against a lamppost to light a cigarette. He didn't recognize the man, but he knew him or rather knew what he was. Paul retreated inside and marched resolutely up the aisle. He was decided and would not be deterred.

He threw a change of clothes and a few things into a small bag. The gun stayed in his pocket. He returned to the church for a last look, sighed and crept out the back way. He dared not take his own car.

Are they watching the airport? Almost certainly, that's no good. Sam. Sam will help me without too many questions.

A mile away he rushed up a stone walkway and rapped on the door of a federalist style brick home. Sam Killebrew welcomed him inside. A short time after he entered, the garage door rolled up and Father Paul left behind the wheel of a nondescript, brown Chevrolet Caprice and headed southwest. In Hartford, he exchanged Sam's Caprice for a rental Buick. He dropped the Chevy's keys into the mail. Sam had another set and agreed to retrieve his car the following day.

CHAPTER 1

Landry carried the bags to car and stowed them in the trunk with the others, wondering why a woman needed so many clothes for only four days.

Dere's jus' some tings men ain't supposed to know, Johnny informed him. *Like how dat one pair of da shoes be beige and one ecru and dey be da same color.*

She must be taking both pairs to be sure she's got all the bases covered, Landry replied.

Now you learnin' Eddie.

Landry sighed and closed the trunk hoping that precluded any more bags from appearing on the front porch. Sighing anew, he lingered in the driveway, hands on his hips, slowly shaking his head. He missed the days of just jumping in the car and taking off. The car in front of him might be a precision driving machine, but he missed his Jeep.

"If it's any consolation, I miss my Porche too," Jazz said lacing her arm through his and resting her head on his shoulder. "Are you sorry?"

Landry looked at her and smiled. "Not a bit. You?"

"No, as long as you remember—"

"It's all my fault. I got it," he said. "I hope Miz Clara will be alright."

"Miz Clara? What about the kids?"

"Lord have mercy on anyone who tangles with those two."

Dey take after dare father, Johnny added.

"Et tu, Johnny," Landry said with a laugh.

His laughter was cut short. Clara stepped out onto the porch and waved for him to come over. He sighed and headed toward her.

I am not putting off this trip, not no way, not no how.

Keep rat on tellin' yoself dat, Johhny cautioned.

"Sheriff, I mean, Ed," Clara began. "There's a man on the phone who needs your help. He says he's a priest."

"Tell him we'll be back, Wednesday," Landry told her.

"But I don't...oh, you go on. I'll take care of it."

"I know you will."

After a final goodbye to the children and yet one more prayer for Miz Clara, Ed and Jazz got into the car headed for "us time" at Mardi Gras. The lush green countryside going by on either side, the soft music and the quiet from the rear seat was working it spell on Jazz. She stretched her arm onto his shoulder and rubbed the back of his neck confirming her impression.

"What's the matter?" she asked.

"Nothing," he replied and gave her a smile. "What could be the matter? We're on our own for Mardi Gras."

"My point exactly," she said. "We are supposed to be having fun and here you are wound up tighter than a cheap watch. What's the matter? Don't tell me it's one of your dreams."

"You're safe there," Landry said. "Do you think we should move? You know, get away from here and not come back?"

"No, why would I? This is home."

"Close your eyes. Go ahead close them. Morgan City, Thibodaux, New Orleans, Burbon Street. What do you see?"

"Okay, so things aren't always easy."

"Aren't always easy? That's putting it mildly. Wouldn't you just like a quiet life like normal people?"

"Normal is boring," Jazz said with a laugh. "You wouldn't like it."

"I used to like it."

"You did? When was that? In Vietnam, or being a sheriff charged with protecting an entire Parish? When I met you, you were far from—I don't want to say normal, let's say ordinary. Johnny saw it. That's why he came to you for help."

"Help?"

"Yes, help. He wanted you to stop him, just not until he was done. You were the only one he could trust to see it didn't happen again."

"But it did happen again, and it's been going on ever since" Landry protested.

Dat's not my fault, Johnny murmured.

Landry could imagine him his bottom lip poked out pouting.

"That's not his fault. It's always gone on," Jazz echoed the sentiment. "It's just that you're such—"

"A sucker," he replied and after a short pause broke into laughter.

"I was going to say good man," she said joining his laughter. "Now, that's better. We're going to have fun, you understand?"

"Yes, ma'am. I do have a question though. It kind of goes to being normal."

"Fire away," Jazz told him.

"Normal people don't get last minute reservations a block off Burbon Street during Mardi Gras and an invitation to ride on a float."

She glanced up at the roof of the car for a moment before looking out the passenger window before she answered.

"That's true," she admitted. "I guess normal people don't have Clara Eddington for a friend and neighbor."

"I see. You know sometimes I get the idea she's had a hand in the way my life has gone since the night we found Delmer."

"Maybe before," Jazz suggested.

"What?"

"Oh nothing, sweetheart," she quickly added.

Landry pushed the phone call to the back of his mind. Jazz seemed willing to let the interruption go. He decided to relax and do the same. He switched the radio to some zydeco and steered the car toward New Orleans. Meanwhile, Jazz steered the conversation in the direction of hotels and plans for their stay. The miles whisked by until they reached Westwego.

"Welcome to W New Orleans, madame," the valet greeted Jazz as he opened her door.

"Good luck with those," Landry told the bellman who arrived to gather their luggage onto a cart.

The man gave Landry a knowing smile and fell in behind them as they stepped inside to the reception desk.

A short time later, Landry opened the door to their room to find Clara Ellington had once again gone overboard. It was not the nice little hotel room Landry expected, but a one-bedroom studio. He walked over to open the doors and look out from their balcony.

"You don't seem surprised by all of this," Landry remarked, spreading his hands out toward the room.

"You know Miz Clara," she replied with a shrug.

"I doubt that more every day. She must have some teacher's pension."

"She lives simply."

"Sure, she does," his skeptical reply was laced with sarcasm.

"Relax, while I unpack," Jazz told him.

Having learned the safest course was to not touch her clothes, Landry dropped down on the king-size bed to watch Jazz unpack her bags. He admired her meticulous folding and hanging of clothes without acquiring a desire to emulate her. The process completed to her satisfaction; she was immediately ready for a night on the town.

"Where are you taking me for dinner?" she asked, rubbing her palms together in front of a huge grin.

"You'll never guess," Landry teased. He had no clue where she wanted to go.

"Pierre Maspero's, really? It's about time," Jazz said.

Ah, I saw that one on the way here.

"Anything for you. It's a short walk on a beautiful evening. A good chance to show off my beautiful wife. Whom, I bet, now wants to change clothes.'

"Of course, and so do you. Good thing I packed for you too."

"How exciting," he quipped. "What am I wearing?"

"I'm glad you asked."

Landry wasn't as glad as she was. It wasn't that he never wore a suit and tie, he just avoided it whenever possible.

Nice shoes, Johnny said.

Shut up, Johnny. These are killing my feet.

When did I buy these shoes," Landry asked aloud.

"Last week, like them? I think wingtips are sexy."

"So, they have a redeeming quality after all."

"Time will tell," Jazz told him with a laugh.

"Shall we go?" he said holding his arm out to her.

Landry ordered Blackened Chicken Jambalaya while Jazz opted for Shrimp and Grits.

"Oh, and the fried alligator appetizer too, please," Jazz added.

"You know I think the entire species is going to rue the day one of them dared attack you," Landry said, giving the waiter a nod to assure him it was true.

Jazz looked up at the waiter. "My bite is worse than my bark."

"I believe you, madame," he replied and hurried away to the sound of their laughter.

"Just so you know," Jazz said. "That whole guess where we're going thing fooled nobody. But it was a nice try."

"I do what I can," he answered.

Jazz did her best to exact a measure of revenge on the order of crocodilia before the main course arrived. The food came a short while later and vanished over the next hour. After paying the check, they wandered out for a stroll among the crowd on Burbon Street before turning back toward the hotel.

"Ah, sure and there's Kelly's," Landry said in a pitifully bad Irish brogue. "And, saints preserve us, right next to me hotel at that. Feel like a pint, luv?"

"If your plan is to ply me with alcohol making me susceptible to your silver-tongued advances," Jazz said. "Let me tell you, the alcohol is unnecessary and time's a wasting."

"Never let it be said that Ed Landry was ever guilty of wasting a lady's time."

Executing a neat arm in arm turn, they entered the hotel and took the elevator to their room. Jazz paused to retrieve a bit of sheer, lacy material and disappeared into the bathroom. The door closed behind her, suddenly opened again and Jazz peeked out.

"Hang your clothes up," she warned.

"I will, but I won't like it," Landry shot back.

"I'll make it worth your while," the reply came through the door.

Landry took off his coat and slipped it onto a hanger before loosening his tie. He pulled the silk from around his neck when there was a knock at the door.

"No," he said. "No, no, no, not this time. Go away."

The knob twisted back and forth

"I said, go away," Landry repeated, but he was walking toward the door as he said it.

Landry twisted the doorknob and was driven back a step when something heavy fell against it. A man dressed in black rolled off the door, attempted a stumbling step inside, and collapsed on the carpet at Landry's feet. Landry turned him over. His breath caught in his throat when he saw the priest's collar.

"Who was—" Jazz began and ducked back inside the bathroom.

She reappeared a moment later wearing a hotel robe and rushed to Landry who was kneeling beside the priest.

"Landry," the priest said through clenched teeth. "They lied. God forgive me. There was never a chance. Witches from the beginning... everything a lie...cover up."

The priest's entire body seized in a titanic convulsion, a grunt forced itself from blue lips, and he was still. Landry placed two fingers to the man's throat."

"He's dead."

CHAPTER 2

Landry gave a quick toss of his head in the direction of their balcony. Jazz, having reclaimed her abandoned evening clothes, followed him out and took the chair he pulled out for her.

"I feel better with more clothes on," she said. "I have a funny feeling that isn't going to last long."

"Having your clothes on or feeling better?" he asked, smiled, and added, "Inquiring minds want to know.

"Feeling better. The clothes are staying on."

"I was afraid of that."

"What is it," Jazz asked. "You've been holding something back since we left home. Let's have it."

"A priest called just before we left. That's what Miz Clara wanted. I told her he could wait until we got back."

"Looks like he couldn't wait."

"Yeah. I don't think these fellas need to know that do you?"

"No way," she agreed.

A few minutes later, a lanky clean-shaven man with wavy brown hair wearing a dark blue suit separated himself from the mob in their room and stepped through the French doors to join Ed and Jazz on the balcony. He had a long straight nose, and a slightly pointed chin though his features were far from sharp. He introduced himself as Lt. Barton Jenks from Homicide.

"You found out who our unexpected guest is yet?" Landry asked.

"We're working on it," Jenks replied. "We could use some help."

"Like we told your men, we've never seen him before."

"Yet you say he knew your name. Any idea how?"

"None you would believe," Landry told him.

"What's that supposed to mean?"

"My husband and I are private investigators," Jazz answered. "Our clients tend to be a little…let's just say odd and leave it at that."

"Let's don't," Jenks countered. "Let's define odd."

"You asked for it," Landry said.

"Odd as in practitioners of voodoo, vampires and other assorted supernatural creatures," Jazz deadpanned.

"Told you," Landry quickly added.

"Let's just say I believe you," Jenks responded with a wry smile. "Don't people troubled by ghosts and evil spirits usually *go to* priests. What's a priest doing coming to you?"

"It is a bit out of the ordinary, isn't it?"

"What exactly did he say again?" Jenks asked.

"They lied. God forgive me. There was never a chance, witches from the beginning…everything a lie…cover up," Landry repeated the words.

"Any idea what lies and cover up he was talking about?"

"Your guess is as good as mine," Landry said.

"I doubt that," the detective replied with a shake of his head.

"Any guesses as to what killed him?" Jazz intervened.

"No, there's no blood, no wound. The coroner should be here soon."

"I'm ex-crime scene," Jazz said. "Mind if I have a look?"

"It's breaking protocol, but at this point, I'll take all the help I can get."

"Hey, I think found something," a voice from the hallway called.

"Don't touch it," Jazz and Jenks said as one.

"What is that, a toothpick?" a patrolman asked, pointing at a sliver of wood lying against the baseboard.

"Too big," the cop next to him replied.

"I'd say it's a dart," Jazz told them. "A poison dart, to be exact. Jenks, there's your murder weapon."

"That means he was shot with it right here in the hall," Landry said.

"Seal off the hotel," Jenks ordered. "And start getting names and interviewing the guests."

"That's probably not necessary," Landry said. "I think somebody followed him here."

"Why would they do that just to kill him?"

"Whoever it was wanted to send us a message," Jazz speculated.

"Who would do that?" the detective asked.

"The list gets longer all the time," Landry answered.

"Who's at the top?" Jenks wanted to know.

"Does the name Marie Dupree ring a bell?"

"Well, as a matter of fact..."

"You're kidding," Landry said when it seemed Jenks wasn't going to say more. "How do you know her?"

"I get around and in this town the name of the voodoo queen just seems to be a part of normal conversation."

"You heard anything lately?" Jazz asked.

"Not since some people ended up dead down by the cemetery on Prytania Street," Jenks replied. "I think you two know the place."

"Too well," Jazz said. "There are ice tongs in the room. I'll get them and get that thing bagged before somebody else gets hurt."

"You think it's still dangerous?"

"Detective, minute amounts, I'm talking micrograms, of tree frog toxins can kill. If that's what was used. Of course, we don't know for sure that's what we're dealing with."

"Do those frogs live in Mexico?" Landry asked.

"I know what you're thinking, but no. The ones I suspect were used here are from Colombia, but they do get smuggled out. Mexico is the easiest way into the country."

"Well, I don't know what he's thinking, fill me in," Jenks urged.

"One of the people that escaped that little disturbance you spoke about, was in Mexico just before everything blew up," Jazz explained.

Detective Jenks steered them back into their room and paused to look at his men working the room."

"Coroner's here," one of the men announced.

Jenks handed Landry his card. "Call me. Let's get together tomorrow for a private conversation. Completely off the record, if you know what I mean."

"Meanwhile, don't leave town?" Landry asked.

"Exactly."

"I thought they'd never leave," Landry confessed.

"That's it? No complains about how this always happens?" What have you done with *my* Ed?

"I told him to wise up. It happens and the thing to do now is to make the best of the few hours we have until dawn."

"I don't like that look it your eye," Jazz said backing away.

"It's working, look."

Jazz glanced back. She was inches from the edge of the bed. She turned her face back to him and smiled. "You get started and there'll be no sleep tonight."

"Sleep's overrated," he replied reaching for her.

The morning light streamed through the french doors that opened onto the patio. Contrary to expectations, they had managed to sleep. Landry put his arm around her waist.

"Turn off that light," Jazz mumbled, turning away from the window.

"That job is above my pay grade," he said. "My job deals in darkness."

"I thought your job was to please your wife."

"That's just one of the perks," he said with a chuckle and nuzzled her ear.

"Feel free to keep that up," Jazz told him. "Because this is another fine mess you got us into. You still owe me a real honeymoon and things aren't looking like this is going to make up for it."

"Since you brought it up," he replied. "What do you think Jenks wants to talk about in private?"

"Obviously it's not something he wants his fellow cops to know. So, I'm betting it's something personal. My guess is that he's a believer."

"In voodoo?"

"Maybe," Jazz replied. "But I think more about things that go bump in the night in general."

Landry looked deeply into her eyes. "Do you trust him?"

"Not yet, you?"

"I want to."

"But?" Jazz said sensing there was more.

"But, if he is a believer in such things, he could be on the other side," Landry said.

"He could be the killer checking to see what the priest might have told us."

"What *exactly* did he tell us?" Landry questioned. "He didn't have a chance because he was lied to, and it was a cover up from the beginning. But who was lying and what were they lying about?"

"And why us?" Jazz added. "Maybe if we find out who he is, we might be able to answer that."

"If only I had a friend who helped me figure out things like this," Landry said.

"Yeah, a kind of guardian angel sort of friend, Jazz said, looking above.

Why you say dat? I don't know. Johnny spoke up.

"You can't ask around?" Landry asked aloud.

You know dat's not how dis works, Johnny countered.

I forgot. You don't do answers.

C'est vrai, dat's rat, rat dere. Maybe you answer da phone, you know something.

"He said something," Jazz said. "What did he say?"

"He said he doesn't know anything, but we should answer the phone."

"Can we wait until it ri—"

The ringing phone cut her off. Landry shrugged and reached for the phone.

"Landry."

"I know I said for you to call me," Jenks said. "But I just found out who the dead priest is. We need to talk. I'm on my way there.

"Not here," Landry replied. "Café Beignet on Royal Street. Thirty minutes."

"I'll be there."

CHAPTER 3

The cloudless morning was warm, touched by a light welcoming breeze. The streets were crowded with a mix of late-night revelers yet to find their way home and tourists eager to begin the new day. Landry wasn't quite sure which group they belonged to. The walk to the café was a short one that was nearly cut shorter. Jazz stepped from the curb to cross Chartres Street. Landry caught her by the arm and dragged her back onto the sidewalk in time to avoid a tow truck moving too fast for the crowded conditions.

"Hey," Jazz scolded.

"Didn't your mama teach you to look both ways before you cross the street?" he joked. "That Yankee nearly got you."

Jazz gave him a sharp look that quickly changed into a smile. "You should be thankful that I don't always do what my mama told me. But thank you."

They arrived at the café where Jenks was seated at a sidewalk table with a steady stream of passersby flowing by him.

"What did he do call us from here?" Landry whispered to Jazz as they approached.

"Must have. It didn't take us that long to dress," she replied.

"Good morning," Jenks greeted them. "Did you sleep well?"

"It's Mardi Gras," Jazz said. "No one sleeps well even without dead priests dropping in."

"True. Sit," the detective said holding out a hand to the empty chairs. "Coffee and beignets are on the way."

"Not a very private spot," Landry commented watching people going by. "But to land a table on the sidewalk, that is an accomplishment.

"My niece owns the café. As for the crowd, we're just part of the scenery. No one will pay us any mind."

"You said that you learned the identity of the priest," Landry reminded him.

"So, I did. But first, here's our coffee."

A sugar covered beignet and a few sips of strong coffee gave a pleasant blush to the morning and their host a willingness to share what he'd learned.

"Okay," Jenks said at last. "Here's what we found out so far about your priest."

"He's not our priest, but go ahead," Jazz told him.

"His name is Rev. Paul Poulard. He is...er...was the parish priest at St. Clement's in Salem, Massachusetts. Yes, *that* Salem, the site of the famous witch trials in the late 1600s. It seems the good Father vanished a few days ago."

"Any ideas on why he crashed our vacation?" Jazz asked.

"I was hoping you'd tell me," Jenks replied.

"Never heard of him," Landry chimed in. "How does a priest just vanish without leaving word with somebody? Didn't he have a mass to say yesterday?"

"I don't know. I suppose," Jenks answered. "I do know that he borrowed a deacon's car on Thursday afternoon and dropped at Hertz in Hartford, Connecticut. He wouldn't tell the deacon where he was going. For what it's worth, I got the impression that the deacon didn't want to know."

"As in he didn't want to lie if someone came looking," Landry said.

"That's my take on it," the detective replied. "Which makes me curious about why a priest colludes with a deacon of the church to suddenly vanish. And, then shows up fifteen hundred miles away at the door of investigators who specialize in the paranormal. Any thoughts?"

Jenks let the silence grow between them while his eyes watched for any signs the pause would prompt Landry to speak. The Landrys simply smiled at him and waited.

“Oh, come on,” Jenks finally said. “I didn’t have to tell y’all any of that. Talk to me.”

“Okay,” Jazz told him. “That’s fair enough. But let’s back up a step. What do you mean when you say paranormal?”

“Well, how about voodoo to start with?

“Religious nonsense,” Jazz quickly replied.

“No, it’s not. I told you that last night. I believe. I’ve been a cop here too long not to.”

“I believe you,” Landry said. “I just don’t know whose side you’re really on. Marie Dupree had an FBI agent in her pocket, why not a local cop too?”

“For all we know, you killed the priest to gain our trust,” Jazz added.

“You’ve got to be kidding me.” Jenks glared at them. “You’re not kidding me, you’re serious. I got no counter for that. I guess we’re done.”

Jenks rose, pushed his chair under the little iron table, and gave them a solemn shake of his head. “I got the bill,” the detective said. “Enjoy your coffee.”

He reached the café door and stepped inside. As the door closed behind him, Landry looked at his wife, arched his eyebrows, and held his palms toward her.

Jazz nodded. “Salem? As much as I hate to say it, go get him.”

Jenks was standing at the register talking to his niece. Landry stepped up behind him and tapped his shoulder.

“Come on back, let’s talk,” Landry said.

Jenks' niece laid a hand on her uncle's arm. "Give us a minute, please," she said.

"Sure thing," Landry replied and headed for the door. As he stepped outside and turned toward their table, he caught sight of Jenks and his niece in animated conversation.

Ho, what's dat dere? Johnny asked.

You could just tell me, Landry replied.

Where da fun in dat?

That's what I thought.

"Everything okay," Jazz asked when he walked up.

"I don't know. His niece kept him back to talk with him and it didn't look like a happy conversation," Landry said. "Then Johnny had to hoot about it which doesn't bode well."

"And, of course, he wouldn't say why."

"You got it," Landry replied. "Looks like we're on our own."

"Here he comes," Jazz whispered.

"Everything alright?" Landry asked when the detective was seated.

Jenks studied their faces long enough to create anticipation that he was going to drop a bomb on the whole deal.

"Okay," he said at last. "Honesty, right? Laronda doesn't think I ought to get involved with you two. Some kind of weird vibration, that's what she says. You both look pretty steady to me though."

"Anything else?" Jazz asked.

"She says Baron Samedi told her to keep me away from you."

"Do you believe her?" Jazz pressed him.

"It's hard not to after that FBI thing," Jenks said. "I knew Fitz. He was a good man."

"Yes, he was," Landry agreed. "Since we're being honest, there are a couple of things you should know. First, that priest called our house yesterday morning."

Jenks drew himself up in his seat and leaned closer.

"Neither of us talked to him," Landry explained. "Our friend who is watching the kids answered. I told her it could wait. She was the only one I know that could have told him where we were staying. The other thing is that on our way here, we were nearly run over by a tow truck carting away a car with Connecticut tags."

"Although, Miz Clara might not be responsible," Jazz added, her head tilted up in thought. "Whoever, or whatever clued him to us in the first place could have been responsible."

"What are you saying? Some voodoo magic sent him here?" Jenks asked. "I've seen some strange stuff, but that's a bit much. Even if it was true, why here? I mean, I get it you two are involved in the paranormal, but why didn't they kill him in Massachusetts?"

"I ask myself that kind of thing all the time," Landry said with a chuckle. "Why me? Why here? Why now?"

"It's true," Jazz spoke up. "He's a real drag that way,"

"What's the answer?" Jenks asked.

Landry shrugged. "Shit happens? That's the best I can come up with anyway."

"You seem to lack the usual skepticism. What has happened to you?" Jazz asked.

"I seemed to remember that, not far from here, some people were torn to shreds by an animal—a big animal. Forensics said it was a big cat or a wolf. There's a lot of strange things go on in this town, but wolves and leopards ain't the usual suspects."

"Who is?" Jazz probed.

"Rougarou, werewolf, crazed lunatic wearing cat claws, voodoo spirit, I don't know. Then we have more than the usual number of dead found around town with holes in their necks and no blood. I haven't interviewed a vampire suspect in any of those yet. But I'm sure it's just a matter of time."

"What if I told you, all of the above?" Jazz said.

"Personal knowledge?" Jenks asked.

"As personal as it can get," she replied leaning closer and meeting his eyes.

"You mean—"

"Don't make her mad," Landry interrupted.

"So, Laronda's strange vibe isn't so strange after all," Jenks said with a shake of his head. "What do we do now?"

"Hopefully, our priest isn't going anywhere," Landry said. "Check out that car. Maybe my wife and I can still salvage today and tomorrow."

"And then?" the detective asked.

"We go to Salem to see how it's all connected," Jazz announced. "But let us know when you find the car. I'd like to check it out."

"Will do. Stay in touch until you leave," Jenks said. "Hell, just stay in touch, period."

CHAPTER 4

Their first stop after leaving the café was a quick stop at their room to call Clara. Though she had promised not to do it, Jazz seemed thrilled with the chance to check on the kids. Landry held the door for her while she rushed inside and went straight to the phone.

"Hello," Clara said above the sound of something hitting the floor in the background.

"Miz Clara are you alright?" Jazz asked.

"Jasmine, dear. Of course I'm alright. Why wouldn't I be?"

"Oh, I don't know, the crashing noise I just heard," Jazz said.

"Just a tower of blocks falling, dear. As much as you want to hear about the children, I suspect you have another reason for calling. Did Rev. Poulard call on y'all this morning?"

"Actually, he showed up last night in a most spectacular fashion. He dropped dead in our doorway."

Landry put his head next to hers and Jazz tilted the phone for him to hear.

"What? Oh, no, that's so sad. They found him then. How did he die? He wasn't bitten, was he?"

"Bitten, no. He was poisoned," Jazz told her. "Who found him?"

"Poison, that's a relief," Clara said.

"Excuse me, *a relief*?" Jazz asked."

"Probably doesn't feel that way to him," Landry said.

"Oh, but I'm sure it does, Edward, given the alternatives,"

"Do you mind explaining?" he asked.

"Of course not. He was from Salem, Mass—"

"Where the witch trials were, yeah, we got that," Landry said.

"Now, Edward, you know it's not polite to interrupt your elders," Clara scolded. "To finish what I was saying, he told me the witches there were after him. They had sent a vampire to condemn him to be one of the undead. Well, they offered him that or suicide."

"Not a pleasant choice," Jazz said.

"Sorry, for interrupting, Miz Clara," Landry apologized.

"You're forgiven. Just remember nothing is so urgent that your manners can be left behind."

"Yes, ma'am. I'll do that," he said. "Any idea why they were after him?"

"He mentioned a book that he had written about the trials proving there really were witches in Salem Village. He said they worked the proceedings so that innocent people were the ones condemned Which, of course, is true. And before you say it, I realize that's not what you were taught in school."

"Any idea where we can find the book?" Landry asked.

"Barnes and Noble, the library, I really don't know," she replied.

"More to the point, Miz Clara, why now?" Jazz wanted to know.

"Something about a steep rise in supernatural activity and his public comments on the subject. I am sorry about interrupting your vacation, but he sounded so desperate. And, Edward, you did tell me to handle it."

"Yes, ma'am, I did. Thank you," Landry replied, stepping away from the phone.

"Okay, he's gone we can talk about the babies now," Jazz told her.

"We are having a great time," Clara said. "You *are* going to finish your vacation, aren't you? I love spending time with them."

"That's the plan, for now, anyway."

An hour later, Landry walked over, tapped his watch, and held it to his ear. Jazz gave him an exasperated look and waved him closer.

"Tell Daddy goodbye," she said and was answered by two small voices in concert.

"Goodbye, see you soon. Love you," Landry said into the phone.

"He's always been an optimist," Clara replied after he stepped away. "Do what you have to do. We're fine here."

"Just how are we going to go to Massachusetts with the kids?" he asked after she hung up.

"Already taken care of," Jazz told him. "Today, we're going sightseeing like the tourists we are."

"Where are we going?"

"You'll see, come on."

Mardi Gras was not only in the air, but it also crowded its way into the shops, the sidewalks and the streets. The ten-minute walk she led him on took twenty. Landry didn't care how long until he realized where they were going.

"No," he said. "I'm not going in there—not again."

"Oh, for me, please," she cajoled. "Look at how sad my eyes are going to be if you don't."

Thinking he could resist this one time, he looked.

"Okay, just to prove to myself that I can," he relented, succumbing to her charm.

"Of course," she replied with a triumphant smile and took his arm.

The New Orleans Historic Voodoo Museum proved more welcoming in the daylight with people pushing their way in and out.

"Why is it that people who live nearby so seldom go to places like this?" Jazz asked.

"Could be because they are always packed with tourists," Landry answered. "Or it could be that the locals are trying to kill you."

"You're safe. Mama Lille is gone forever," Jazz assured him.

"Is she?"

"Yes...and no."

"That's what I thought. Hey, look at that," he said walking toward a framed display of dolls."

"Checking for anybody in particular?" a woman asked.

"More like who is absent," Landry commented still staring at the display.

"I can help you if you need a special one," the woman offered.

Landy looked at her for the first time. She was smiling at him, but there was something vicious in her straight white teeth and piercing brown eyes. Jazz pushed closer to his side.

"He has all the help he needs," Jazz said.

The woman forked Jazz the sign of the evil eye. "Bitch."

Jazz growled deep in her throat and the woman fled, shoving her way through the crowd.

"I have to watch you every minute," Jazz teased.

"That red fellow with the horns, the bottle of rum and big cigar over there," Landry said pointing at another display. "Is that Baron Samedi?"

"No, he usually has a skeletal face," she replied. "He does like rum and cigars though. Did you like the dolls?"

"Only that none of them looked like me," Landry replied.

"Okay, I have an idea, follow me."

"Anywhere," Landry told her.

"Now that's an invitation to trouble if I ever heard one," Jazz said pulling him along toward the exit.

You put dat boot in your mouth now, Johnny said with a laugh.

Fifteen minutes later, they arrived at a small sign on the sidewalk that proclaimed the place to be Bloody Mary's Tours, Haunted Museum and Voodoo Shop.

"I thought we were on vacation," Landry groused after they were inside.

"We are. This will be fun," Jazz assured him. "It's supposed to really be haunted."

"Not my idea of fun," Landry said.

"Oh, quit," she scolded. "Over that way, come on."

"A voodoo doll workshop?" Landry said. "*This* has possibilities."

"See, I told you."

"So, if I build one that looks like you, will I be able to work my will on you?"

"You already do th—"

"What is it?" Landry started to turn to see what she was looking at.

"Don't look, yet," she whispered. "Okay, take a quick peek over your right shoulder. Near the door.

He did as instructed. "The lady from the voodoo museum."

A scream momentarily froze everyone in the room.

"What the hell is that?" a man shouted seconds before several people stampeded for the door.

Cameras flashed from every direction. A black mist floating about a foot off the floor drifted towards Landry and Jazz. Anger radiated off it in waves that sent the rest of the tourists flying for the door. The specter slowly took on the shape of a man. He raised his arm and pointed at Landry. When he did the voodoo dolls jumped from their display to the floor and the specter abruptly vanished.

"Perhaps we should go now," Jazz suggested.

"Good idea," Landry agreed and placed his doll making materials back where he found them.

They moved toward the exit as a fresh stream of people hearing the wild talk on the sidewalk flowed in to get a look. A buzz of excited, yet muted conversations surrounded them, and fingers pointed as they reached the door.

"Wait," a woman's voice rose above the buzz. "Please, sir, ma'am, don't go. Please wait."

They stopped short of the door and slowly turned to see a woman in a tropical print dress and bright red tignon headed toward them. The woman was very solid and rather bulky with ebony skin. When she reached them, she paused to catch her breath before speaking.

"That was not one of ours," she said, pointing back the way Landry had come and shaking her head.

"You've lost me," Landry said.

"Can we talk in my office? I'd love to explain."

"I think that might be helpful," Jazz said.

"The woman turned around and took a few steps, Jazz following closely behind her.

"One moment," Jazz said touching the woman on the arm and looking back. "Ed?"

Landry had not moved. "Are you sure it's a good idea to go back that way?"

"It'll be fine," the woman said. Her voice dropped to a breathy whisper as she added, "I hope."

"It will," Jazz answered with a smile.

The woman eyes widened a bit with the knowledge that Jazz heard her. Undeterred, she waved for Landry to follow.

"If you please, sir."

Landry shrugged and complied, falling in behind the women. She led them up a stairway to an upper room. The room itself was part of the museum used for the seances and card readings. A small round table covered with a red velvet cloth sat in the center of the room. Landry and Jazz sat opposite the woman.

"You were going to explain," Jazz said when their hostess seemed lost in thought.

"Yes, excuse me my spirit is very unsettled. As I said, the ghost that appeared was not one of ours. That is, I have never seen him before."

"One of yours, I'm still not sure what you mean," Landry said. "You have your own ghosts on exhibit. How does that work?"

"It's not trickery, if that's what you're getting at. We don't do that here. However, on this section of Rampart Street, there are at least a dozen known ghosts. People see them all the time."

"Including you?" Landry asked.

"Very definitely."

"I'm assuming you are Bloody Mary," Jazz said.

"Yes, and no."

"You see," Landry spoke up. "that's my problem with all you spiritualists, voodoo worshippers, and ghostly types in general. You can never just answer a question straight out."

"What I'm was trying to say is that Bloody Mary is more a stage name. My real name is Anne Marie Bass. Is that better?"

"Much," Landry replied.

"You'll have to excuse Ed," Jazz told her. "I kind of made him come along."

"You were hoping for something like this, weren't you?" Landry asked.

"He's kind of a magnet," Jazz explained to Anne.

"I have to agree. Tell me, what did you stir up in my shop?" Anne asked.

"You tell me," Landry replied.

"Someone very angry with you. A spirit very close to the center of the spirit world," Anne stated and shrugged.

"Well, you asked," Jazz told him.

CHAPTER 5

They left the haunted museum a short while later, a trifle unsettled at the psychic's impression. Her efforts to shake up the spirit world a success, Jazz abandoned her walking tour of the city's shadowy side. She decided to switch to its other claim to fame—food. Their walk back toward the hotel led them along Louis Armstrong Park and then south along Conti past a place that caught Landry's eye.

"Let's eat here," Landry said. "The name seems to fit."

"Déjà Vu? Hmm, okay," Jazz replied. "I'm hungry and you're right, the name *does* fit."

The Déjà Vu was painted a pale salmon with dark green doors. Wrought iron railings closed in the second story balcony. After a short wait, they found seats at the bar. They had not been there long when a familiar voice interrupted their conversation.

"I guess that little stop at Bloody Mary's didn't go so well," Barton Jenks said.

"Are you following us?" Landry asked. "Because if so, you're good at it and two, I don't like it."

"Let's just say I'm keeping tabs on you. Which, by the way is not difficult. You seem to cause a stir even amid all the commotion of Mari Gras." Jenks turned to the woman beside him. "You remember my niece. Those folks are leaving, let's grab the table and I'll properly introduce you."

"What about the—"

"Staff?" Jenks finished for Landry and flashed his badge at the busboy. "No problem. Come on."

"That never worked in Lockett," Landry told Jazz.

"There's always an empty table in Lockett," she replied.

"Ed and Jazz Landry, meet my niece, Claudette Chavais.

"I never thought I'd be doing this," Claudette said as she shook Landry's hand. "The infamous Ed Landry."

"Infamous?" Landry said with a tilt of his head and arched eyebrows. "I don't think anyone's every called me that before."

"You're quite well known in certain circles," Claudette assured him. "Mama Lille is not forgotten. Marie Dupree may think she's assumed her grandmere's place, but it is not so, not yet."

"So the enemy of your enemy is your friend, is that it?" Jazz asked extending a hand.

Their hands joined across the table and the two women seemed locked in a staring match that lasted longer than their companions liked. They broke the connection with matching sharp intakes of breath.

"And this one, she gives me the frissons," Claudette said rubbing her arms. You know what she is, don't you?"

"And it's real?" Jenks asked.

"Oh it's real. I don't know how it lasts so long, but it's real," Claudette confirmed.

"Mama Lille's handiwork," Jazz said. "Her curse has become my blessing."

"What did Bloody Mary look like?" Claudette asked.

"A slightly overweight mixed-race woman, maybe in her thirties," Jazz answered.

"That wasn't Bloody Mary, the shop owner," Jenks told them. "She's a blonde, white woman."

"Then who was it?" Landry asked.

"She may have been more solid, but she's a ghost every bit as much as the other."

"I got the impression the ghost who caused all the trouble was the dead priest," Landry said.

"I doubt it," Claudette told him. "But I think you were meant to think so."

"By whom?" he asked.

"Marie Dupree.'

"But why? What does Marie want with me?" Landry asked.

"That's the key," Claudette informed him. "Marie always wants something. She's up to something big. She wants your unwitting help. My guess is to betray her allies."

"What allies would those be?" Jazz asked.

"I don't know. He's a mystery, and a powerful one," Claudette said. "He's not here. Marie goes to meet him and returns a little more powerful every time."

"She's getting something from him, but she wants it all," Jazz replied. "That's Marie, all right. And who better to cause her friend trouble than Ed."

"I think you're right," Claudette said.

"Then we know where she's going," Landry spoke up.

"And we know what she's after," Jazz added.

"The book," they said in unison.

"What book?" Claudette asked.

"I'm going to be blunt," Landry told her. "You don't need to know, and I don't want you to know." He turned to Jazz. "He was here, at Marie's house when we were there."

"Is Marie in town now?" Jazz asked.

"Yes, that's why I agreed to meet you."

"You could have told us that this morning," Landry said.

Claudette gave him a victorious smile. "You didn't need to know then."

"Fair enough," Landry said. "Just remember which side you're on."

"And what side would that be?" Claudette snapped. "If you think anyone involved in this cares for anything but their own best interest, then you're a fool, Ed Landry."

Claudette pushed back from the table, stood, and walked away into the crowd without looking back.

"I'd better go see about her," Jenks said and rushed out after her.

"That was interesting," Landry offered.

"What that he went chasing after his *niece* or that you haven't ordered for us yet?"

"You mean they're..."

Landry's finger rapidly went back and forth between where Jenks and Claudette had been sitting. Jazz nodded at him and smiled.

"But he's...I mean she's really young enough. Wow, nice work detective."

Jazz fixed him a dubious look. "You really want to go with that comment?"

"Ah, no. I want to order," he said wielding the menu as a shield.

"Good," she said, her hand coming to rest on his thigh. "Where are we going after lunch?"

Landry looked up at the tall glass windows and metal latticework and shook his head.

"The library wasn't quite what I had in mind," he said. "Do you really think this is necessary?"

"Where else are we going to learn about witches and witch trials?"

"And I thought you loved me."

"I do, that's why we're going together," Jazz said. "I know your history with librarians."

"I'd say we are safe, but after the way the day has gone so far, you never can tell. Let's go."

They gathered an armful of books and found a table to spread them out on.

"Learn anything you didn't already know?" Landry asked about an hour into their search.

"Not until just this moment," Jazz answered. "We're doing this all wrong."

"Wrong how?"

"What do you know about the Salem Witch Trials?" Jazz asked.

"Same as anybody else,' he replied. "Some girls started having convulsions and such. They blamed them on being bewitched and began pointing fingers. Hysteria set in and eventually took over. It wasn't the first time some of them were accused of witchcraft. Close to twenty were hanged, one guy was pressed to death and more died in jail. Later the governor of the colony dissolved the court, pardoned and released those still held. The trials were later deemed unlawful, names were cleared and restitution made to the heirs."

"Right. And what you read just confirmed that."

"Yeah, why shouldn't it? That's what happened."

"Is it really? Have you ever collected evidence and have a court throw it out?"

"Yeah, so?"

Did that evidence dissolve into thin air because the court refused to look at it?"

"Of course not, what's you point? I know you have one."

"There was evidence at the trials," Jazz said. "Folks like Cotton and Increase Mather wanted it thrown out. They called it spectral evidence—evidence from dreams and visions. I recall the dream of this Louisiana sheriff that landed us in a fine mess one time. It must not have been true."

"We want to accept the discrediting of the judges and witnesses because it fits our denial of the existence of witchcraft," Landry said. "We have been reading to accept the conclusions, not question them."

"Exactly. No one ever questions the "judgmental" hatred of the Puritans. It is easier to accept than the existence of witches. But what if they were right?"

"Then, by discrediting them after the fashion of the trials," Landry added. "It was assured no one would ever dare think witches are real. Those who do are forever labeled as crazies."

"Like those who believe in rougarous," Jazz said. "That's what Rev. Poulard's book is about. He must have put forth some sound arguments and needed to be silenced."

"Which brings us back to why us? What did he expect us to do?"

"He said something about never having a chance, that it was a lie," Jazz said. "If we could figure out what he meant by that, maybe we would know."

CHAPTER 6

Making a pact to spend the rest of the day on the vacation they came for, they took a taxi back to the hotel. The streets were alive with people decked out in costumes and layers of purple, gold and green beads. None of them seemed to have a care in the world.

"Amazing, isn't it?" Landry asked.

"It's Mardi Gras," Jazz explained.

"I know," he said. "But I meant all those lives being lived out there. All going their own way, each with his or her own thoughts, desires, and hopes. All of it going on at once. Ever wonder what goes on in all those heads in any given minute?"

"On rare occasions, yes. I'm more than a little surprised to hear you wondering about it—at least right at this moment."

"I have my moments."

"You do indeed. That might be why I love you."

"Only might be?"

"Better take what you can get."

The laughter they shared at the comment ended abruptly. Jazz seized his arm in a vise-like grip.

"What?" Landry asked.

"I thought I...never mind, it was nothing."

"You saw something." Landry pressed her. "What was it?"

"It was nothing. A fleeting glimpse, too fast to be sure of anything."

"What are you not sure you saw, then?"

"Father Poulard."

"Impossible, we're on vacation," Landry said.

"You're right," Jazz agreed. "Just imagining things."

The last few minutes of the ride passed in silence. When they arrived, Landry went around to open her door and pay the driver.

"Maybe you should call home," he said while searching his wallet for the fare.

"You're not putting me off, are you?"

"Not at all," he replied. "I think it would make you happy to hear the kids' voices."

"Ah, trying to get on my good side."

"Can't blame a guy for trying.'

"I can, but not this time," she said stepping over to kiss him.

They continued, arm in arm, to their room where they shared a phone call to Miz Clara and the children. The happy voices from Lockett were received with a mix of emotions familiar to parents away from home. Relief that the house was still standing, mingled with joy that everyone was having fun and touched with disappointment that they weren't missed as much as they hoped. Relief won out and they decided the time to relax as overdue.

Landry ordered a bottle of wine. Just for luck, he crossed his fingers when answering the knock at the door. He breathed again when it was only room service. They sat together on the balcony sipping wine, lost to the world for the moment. They knew it would not last, but savored it, and each other, while it did.

"Dare we go out to dinner?" Jazz asked.

"Sure, we aren't scared."

"We're not?"

"Nope. Mostly because we know there's no place to hide and we have each other."

"That's almost romantic, not quite, but almost," she teased.

"Casual tonight?"

"*Certainment, cher.*"

"Mmm, it does something to me when you speak French," Landry said.

"*We are going out,*" she reminded him.

"Yes, but we are coming back too."

"My turn to pick the place," Jazz said.

"I don't understand men who say their wife never knows where she wants to eat."

"That's because you're blessed with me."

"Is that what it is? Okay, where are we going?"

"Not far."

"I *am* blessed. Lead the way."

A short time later, after pressing their way through a mass of revelers, they arrived at the corner of Bourbon and Conti. They stepped inside a long narrow restaurant. A center aisle was lined on each side with rows of tables. They claimed one just inside the door with a view of the street.

"Okay, I'm going to agree that you are blessed," Jazz told him. "How we can step into a restaurant on Bourbon Street the night before Mardi Gras and there just happens to be a prime table available. That's not me."

"Blind dumb luck," Landry assured her.

"I'll believe it if you do," Jazz replied, with a smile.

"Yeah, I don't buy it either. I'm not going to complain though."

"I'm not complaining. I'm waiting for the other shoe to drop."

"I hope you're not too hungry," Landry said with a nod of his head toward the window. "I think it just did."

"Can I get you something to drink?" a smiling twenty-something woman asked.

"I have a feeling we're going to need it," Jazz told her. "But we can't stay."

She and Landry were quickly on their feet and rushing for the door eager not to lose the two women who were their quarry. They had crossed paths with them earlier in the day. Seeing Claudette and the woman from the Voodoo Museum together was more of a coincidence than even Landry could joke about.

The crowd was both a shield and an obstruction. The women were walking with purpose pushing through the crowd at a much faster pace than the sightseers. Ed and Jazz struggled to keep up and still hang back enough not to catch their eye.

"Maybe we trusted Jenks too soon," Landry said.

"I don't think so. Marie is always working an angle to get what she wants. I think with his niece, it's a case of takes one to know one."

"Could be, but what is Claudette after?"

"Sending Marie on a permanent vacation?"

"That makes sense. Any guesses about where they might be going?"

"Voodoo Museum," Jazz said with a laugh.

"Bite your tongue," he said and looked up. "Lord don't let it be the museum."

"Your prayer was answered," Jazz said when their quarry continued on Chartres past Dumaine Street."

When you gonna learn to beware what you ask for? Johnny asked.

"Oh joy," Landry answered aloud. "Johnny says it's worse."

"Oh joy," Jazz repeated. "Does he know where?"

"Probably, but he never tells."

"What's this?" Jazz asked pointing ahead. "Nothing but girl's night out. We put off dinner for this. Oh crap."

Jazz threw out an arm to stop Landry.

"What?" Landry said, searching for trouble. "What am I missing?"

Dey goin' to church, Eddie. Dat big church rat dere.

"What's the big deal with the church?" Landry asked Jazz.

"That's the Urusalines Convent," Jazz answered,

grabbing his chin, and turning his face to hers. "Famous for miracles and its vampires. And those two with them don't look like miracles."

"I don't know how they are going to do it, but it looks like they're going inside," Landry said.

"Well, we're not," Jazz added. "We find a place and wait to see what happens."

"I'm beginning to think we should have gone to Mardi Gras in Mamou."

"Too late for that. Over there by the brick wall," Jazz directed.

They ducked between a house and a wall that enclosed a small garden courtyard. Slipping into the shadow of a parked van, they waited. They were old hands at a stake out, but hunger and the desire to try to get in a little more vacationing was trying their patience. Landry's stomach rumbled and he placed a hand over it to still the noise.

"Quiet over there," Jazz scolded. "You want to give us away?"

"You're beyond that point," a voice behind them said.

The owner of the voice was a shapely young redhead wearing a dress cut deeper than was decent and slit to the hip. She gave them a toothy smile that showed off her long canines.

"It's not polite to lurk in the dark and spy on people," the woman said.

Jazz growled and took a step forward. The woman raised both palms.

"We don't want trouble," she said. "Why don't we go somewhere. You can get something to eat, and we'll talk."

"We?" Jazz said. "And who is 'we'?"

"You've met Claudette and her friend. "I'm Delphine. Shall we go?"

"And if we say, 'no'?" Landry asked.

"Let's don't think about that. Let's concentrate on a

new...uh...friendship, shall we?"

"Curiosity killed the cat," Jazz said. "But then, I'm no cat. Let's go."

CHAPTER 7

The MRB Bar was a short distance from the river. Much to the Landrys delight, they had a fine kitchen. Oysters St. Philip and chicken fried alligator sandwiches were delivered at record speed. Landry thought Voodoo Blackened Lager sounded good. Jazz chose something called a frozen Green Thang. Claudette and her friend from the Voodoo Museum, whose name was Juliet, joined Jazz in the frozen concoction. Delphine and Emmeline deferred saying they never drank—alcohol and tittering at their little joke. Landry brought the cordial atmosphere to an abrupt end.

"What do you people want?" he said skewering Claudette with his eyes.

"I thought you knew better," Claudette answered in her best Southern lady voice. "That's not how we begin to discuss business. It's not polite."

"Considering I'd put a stake through any of you without a second thought," he replied. "I think that's about as amicable as things are going to get."

Delphine jumped to her feet with a hiss, fire glowing in her eyes. Jazz laid a hand on the vampire's arm and shook her head.

"He can be a real as—ass, sometimes," Jazz explained with a smile. "Unfortunately, he is serious. I've seen him do it. Let's don't pretend we're going to be friends."

Delphine slowly settled back into her chair.

"Then get to the point, sorry about the pun, Delphine," Claudette spoke up. "Can we be allies, at least for a time?"

"That depends on what you want and what it is going to cost us," Landry answered.

"We offer Marie Dupree and her priest killing friends," Claudette responded.

"That's only half an answer," Jazz reminded her.

"We offer peace," Juliet said.

"I don't think that's yours, to give," Landry replied.

"We're all involved in this," Claudette said with a sweep of her hand toward her friends."

"I didn't mean just Juliet," Landry clarified. "I meant all of you."

"I agree, Jazz said. "Perhaps you'd better explain what you mean by peace."

"Barton has told me about you," Claudette confessed. "I told him y'all weren't buying the 'niece' line. I say that so you know he has told me all he knows. You're still a bit of a sheriff, Mr. Landry. Though vigilante might be the better word."

"I like it," Landry interrupted with a chuckle.

"Yes, well, it might surprise you that I don't consider that a bad thing." She held up a hand to prevent an answer. "Mama Lille and her granddaughter have been dabbling in things that give voodoo a bad name."

"Drugs, selling people, old fashion protection rackets," Juliet added.

"And you don't?" Landry asked.

"No," Claudette snapped leaning closer to him. "We don't and we're not going to. Those things will go on once we're rid of Marie, but we can't—won't try to do it alone."

"Someone will inevitably step in," Jazz said.

"Of course they will," Claudette assured her. "We intend to see those who do replace Marie be handled by the police and that *our* friends are protected from those criminals."

"I see," Landry said. "How does the make peace for

us?"

"Your lives won't be interrupted," Juliet said. "Not by what goes on in New Orleans anyway."

"What about those two?" he said, pointing at Delphine and Emmeline.

"*We* have been here for almost three hundred years. Long before the silly men in that movie," Delphine answered.

"So now that we know that," Landry said. "What? We just turn a blind eye?"

"Don't you do that now? Barton seems to think most of your business has nothing to do with the...er...unusual here. It takes a priest dropping dead in your hotel room to get you involved in hunting the supernatural in New Orleans."

"Okay," Jazz agreed. "You have a point there. So, are you saying that if we don't help you that you'll change that?"

"We do know where you live," Claudette said.

"All the more reason to eliminate you before bothering about Marie," Jazz countered.

"We cannot be eliminated, as you put it, so easily," Delphine insisted. "Besides, there's no time for that."

"If that's the case," Landry said. "You better tell us what you're holding back."

"Allies?" Claudette extended her hand.

Ed looked at Jazz who nodded. "Allies."

Ed and Jazz left the bar about two hours ahead of its 4 am closing time. The streets weren't deserted, but the foot traffic had diminished, and the going was easier. Twenty minutes later they were back in their room somewhat better informed, but not any happier.

"Did we just make a pact with the devil?" Landry asked.

"Not really. We bought some time and another chance to destroy that book. Make no mistake about it though, Claudette wants it as bad as Marie."

"And there's no way we can let any of them live knowing where they can find our children."

"Right," Jazz agreed. "Kill 'em all and let God sort 'em out."

"It's the only way. We're going to need help."

"You're thinking Miz Clara?"

"Miz Clara." Landry nodded and lifted his bottle of beer. "I don't know if it's too late or too early, but I say we bring her in now."

"Knowing her, I wouldn't be surprised if she's sitting by the phone waiting."

"You call," Landry said.

"Coward."

It turned out that Jazz was right. Her voice clear and sharp, Clara Ellington answered on the second ring. Jazz looked at her husband and mouthed, I told you. Landry went to stand beside her and listen in.

"Settle a bet," Jazz said. "Were you by the phone waiting for us to call?"

"Of course not, dear," Clara replied. "I was making tea and waiting for something to happen. What *has* happened?"

"We just had a lovely evening with a would-be voodoo queen and a pair of vampires."

"You two always have the best times."

"Not how I'd put it Miz Clara," Landry told her.

"Hello, Sher—Ed, you know you wouldn't have it any other way. Now, tell me, how I can help?"

There's trouble in the Crescent City," Jazz said. "Our old friend Marie Dupree is facing a revolt while she's staging one of her own."

"Be a little more specific, dear. I'm good but I'm not that good. Start with Father Poulard."

"I may call in some help," Clara said after Jazz's tortuous explanation was complete. "Although I don't look for any trouble on this front until the business in Salem is over. We'll be on guard nevertheless."

"I wish we didn't have to be away from the children so long."

"I know you miss them, dear. They miss you too, but like their parents, they are tough troopers. Maybe tougher than any of us yet realize."

Later, Jazz lay awake turning Clara's words over in her mind.

Like Johnny, Miz Clara doesn't always tell all she knows—or suspects.

CHAPTER 8

Landry lay, eyes closed, listening to Jazz breathing beside him. Careful not to wake her, he rolled onto his side to face her. Nature's call was urgent, but not enough to tear him away from this sight. New Orleans and Mardi Gras drew millions. This woman beside him was all the beauty, wonder, and excitement he ever wanted.

If it took voodoo, vampires, and rougarous to bring her into my life, it was worth it.

Dat's some true rat dere, Johnny spoke up.

You know it's even worth you hanging around inside my head, Landry replied. *Why do you hang around, Johnny? Why not go on to heaven? I'd leave you for a ticket to paradise.*

Sure, you would, Eddie. Just like you did when you had me in your jail. Just like you did when you knew what I was. Besides, who says I'm goin' to heaven and who says dis ain't it?"

Hang around me? You got to be kidding.

Why dat? I like you Eddie. Dere's worse things.

I suppose so. Tell me, though, if I ever get there, will I be able to give straight answers?

Dere's no fun in dat.

"And you think baiting me is fun?" Landry unintentionally said aloud.

"I like it," Jazz answered, startling her husband.

Johnny joined her in a laugh at his expense.

"I didn't mean to wake you," Landry said. "It slipped out."

"What were you and your fairy godfather talking

talking about?" Jazz asked.

Now dat's not funny, Johnny said.

It was Landry's turn to laugh. "I don't think he likes his new title."

"He'll get used to it," Jazz assured him. "But there's something I want to know, Ed Landry."

"What's that?"

"Now that I'm awake, what are you going to do about it?"

Landry threw an arm around her, drew her next to him and kissed her.

"Good choice," she told him when their lips parted. "Bye, Johnny."

"I hate to tell you this," Jazz said later. "But you need to get dressed. You have a float to ride.

Landry checked his watch, jumped out of bed and began to rummage through his drawer.

"It's not in there, sweetheart," Jazz told him. "Go shower and I'll get it for you."

When Landry emerged from the bathroom, he found his clothes had magically been laid out on the bed. He held the shirt and vest up inspecting it.

It is Mardi Gras, he reminded himself.

He slipped his arms into the gold silk shirt, pulled on green slacks and buttoned on his purple vest.

Ho, now dere's a look for you, Johnny hooted.

How do you know when to reappear? Landry asked. *Makes me wonder if you're ever really gone.*

C'est un mystère, dat's for sure.

"You make that look good," Jazz said, returning from the bathroom wrapped in a towel.

"Can't hold a candle to what you do for a towel."

"Well, I'm trading it for this," she said holding up an emerald green dress.

"Wow, best sight I've seen in this town. But where are your beads?" he asked.

"Oh I'm sure some good-looking men will throw me

some."

"Maybe this leaving you alone and riding on a float isn't such a good idea."

"You're safe. Besides I'm not wearing this now," she said retreating to the bathroom.

She emerged a few moments later in jeans and shimmering gold blouse.

"How come you get to dress like that and I'm..." His voice gave way to a wave of his hands over his clothes.

"Get your hat. Oh, and don't forget this," she said holding up a white mask, the eyes, nose and mouth highlighted in bold black lines.

"I'm not wearing that thing on my face until I have to," he said, donning the purple fedora and taking the mask from her hand.

The taxi arrived at the door only moments after Ed and Jazz. The four-mile trip down the crowded streets to the staging area on City Park Avenue seemed to take forever. When they got there, Jazz kissed Landry and pushed him out of the cab.

"I'll be at Canal and St. Charles, and I expect some beads," she told him.

"That's hours from now. What are you going to do until then?"

"Shop undisturbed. Haven't you forgot something?"

"Sorry," he said, leaning in to kiss her.

"That was nice, but I meant this," she replied, holding out his mask.

"How will you recognize me with that on?"

"I'll manage. Now, close the door. I have money to spend."

Landry pushed the door closed to the sound of the driver's laughter. Jazz gave him a wave and they were gone.

***

Jazz had the taxi drop her back at the hotel. She *was* going shopping—but for information. She paid the driver, watched the car vanish down Chartres, and set out for the Café Beignet. When she turned the corner onto Royal, she wasn't surprised to see Jenks' unmarked car parked on the street. What caught her by surprise was the feeling of being watched even while being jostled about by a crowd of people.

She walked past the café before stopping to look over the people on the street. When the sidewalk provided no useful information, she lifted her eyes to the upper floors. A fleeting shadow atop the shop across the street piqued her curiosity, but the feeling didn't go away. Deciding to play it out, she returned to the café and stepped inside.

Jenks was standing near the register trying to carry on a conversation with Claudette who was scrambling to wait on customers. Claudette nodded in Jazz's direction and Jenks looked her way. Jazz started over to meet the detective. Claudette handed him a tray with coffee and beignets. Jenks waved for Jazz to follow him to the courtyard where he plucked a Reserved sign from a table and pulled out a chair for her.

"Where's Landry?" he asked.

"With the Krewe of Endymion. I'm meeting him later."

"Meanwhile, you were hungry?"

"Meanwhile, I am doing a bit of recon."

"Recon? I'm afraid I don't understand," Jenks said. "What are you up to?"

"How much do you know about your girlfriend?" She held up a hand to stop him. "Don't pretend you don't know what I'm talking about."

Head bowed, Jenks' eyes rose toward her, and his face flushed.

"It's the 90s, Barton. No one cares that you two are playing around. Wait, are you married?"

"Lord no," shock hijacked Jenks' voice.

Her laughter brought a scowl to his face. "Then, lighten up. How well do you know Claudette and her...uh...pastimes, besides you, that is?"

"I still don't know what you're getting at," Jenks said with a touch of irritation.

"Very well, then. Let me make it plain. Your lady friend is heavily into voodoo. In fact, she'd love to step up. She asked us to help her overthrow the voodoo queen of New Orleans."

"Obviously, I don't know her as well as I thought," Jenks told her. "I mean, I know she practices voodoo. I'm not particularly religious myself. I figure one is about like another. I don't buy all the old horror movie stuff about zombies and sticking pins in dolls though. As far as the rest goes, well, she's always struck me as ambitious. So, I can understand her wanting to get to the top. Just what does she want from you?"

"She thinks her rival had something to do with the murder of the priest," Jazz explained.

"And you and Landry are supposed to do what about that?"

"Cause trouble between Marie Dupree and her friends," Jazz answered. "I think we're to act as a distraction. I get the impression that Claudette hopes it comes to more than that, but she'll take what she can get."

"Will it come to more than that?"

"It usually does," Jazz said. "I think Claudette knows that. What she doesn't know is Landry. He's a Marine and 'kill 'em all' is often his solution to problems."

"Understandable at times," Jenks said with a nod of his head. "But it's still kind of an odd attitude for a sheriff."

"None of the type of people we're talking about are ever going to trial."

"Why not?"

"Because, in the minds of sane jurors, they don't exist. However, cops planting evidence and trumping up bogus charges do. Isn't that right, Claudette?"

Jenks whirled around and looked up at his girlfriend standing at his shoulder.

"I'm afraid she's right," Claudette agreed slowly nodding her head. I guess it's time we had a talk."

"I'll give you two some time," Jazz said, rising from her seat.

"Don't bother," Claudette replied with a wave of her hand. "I'm not going to tell him anything you don't know."

She was right. The conversation was brief and to the point. Claudette laid out the hidden parts of her past and her plans for the future. When she finished, Jenks brushed it off with a 'nobody's perfect' shrug and a grin.

You neglected to mention your vampire friends from the convent, Jazz silently scolded.

Her thoughts were interrupted by the arrival of another of the café staff.

"Miz Claudette, ma'am," the elderly woman said. "There's a phone call for you. I think you'd better take it."

Janks and Jazz watched her go. Before either of them could say a word, Jenks' phone buzzed. He pulled it from his pocket, flipped it open and raised the antenna.

"Jenks," he barked into it. "I'll be right there."

He put the phone back into his pocket.

"I got to go. We got a dead body," he said as Claudette came rushing back into the courtyard.

"It's Juliet," Claudette cried, tears in her eyes. "She's dead."

"I'd better go with you," Jazz told the detective.

"I'm going too," Claudette insisted.

CHAPTER 9

Claudette led the way through the bookstore and up the stairs to Juliet's apartment. Jenks flashed his badge to clear the final obstacle and led the way in. The room was decorated in eclectic yard sale chic accented by voodoo veves only some of which Jazz recognized.

Juliet's body was sprawled on her bed. Claudette pushed her way by Jenks to look at the body. With a gasp, she rushed from the room. Jazz felt she should go after her but wanted a look at whatever sent Claudette fleeing. To her surprise, it was not blood and guts. Juliet's face was frozen into a blue-lipped rictus of abject terror. She'd only seen it once before, but once was enough. She turned in pursuit of Claudette.

She found the café owner sitting on the sofa sobbing into her hands. Settling down beside her, Jazz put an arm around her shoulders. She waited until the tears subsided and Claudette was ready to talk.

"Did you see her face?" Claudette asked in hushed tones. "My God it was awful."

"Yes, it was. I'm sorry you had to go through that," Jazz replied. "I take it you've never seen anything like that before."

"Lord no. What could do—*that*?"

"What I have to tell you may sound cold and callous," Jazz began. "But you asked, and you need to know exactly what we're dealing with."

"What are you saying?"

"I'm saying this is Marie Dupree's doing, and you would do well to reconsider the little revolt you've started. I believe Marie has just told you the same thing. You're not ready for that kind of voodoo. The fact that you've never seen it tells me Marie's power is growing. Mama Lille ignored that fact and paid dearly for it. Don't make the same mistake."

"But...but I can't just let her—"

"Get away with it," Jazz finished for her. "We don't intend to let her. In order to make that happen, you've got to quit playing games with us. Where's Marie and what's she up to—the truth, the whole truth, this time. What did you do?"

"After we met with you and Landry, we called a meeting of friends in the community. You know just to talk things over." Claudette was careful not to make eye contact. "We may have hinted Marie was straying from pure voodoo.'

"Hey, Jazz. Come take a look at this," Jenks called from the bedroom.

Jazz waved and Claudette followed her with hesitant steps, keeping her eyes on the floor. Jenks pointed at a scrap of paper near the head of the bed.

"What do you make of that?" he asked.

"Obviously part of a larger note that Juliet burned," Jazz said and lifted Juliet's hand. "Hold on a second. There are no matches, no lighter, but her fingertips have been burned. She was holding it while it burned. And what's that smudge on the floor? Looks like something burned a small hole all the way through the wood."

Jazz looked at Claudette. No words passed between them, but Jazz's expression clearly asked a question. Claudette seemed to read it plainly. Her hands trembled a bit and she let out a long breath.

"The message caught fire while she was reading it. It's a spell that Marie was using before she left."

"That did not come in the mail," Jazz told Jenks. "Somebody delivered it. Somebody she would open the door for."

"It could be anyone," Claudette said. "It only activates when the intended victim opens it—that is, breaks the seal on it."

"There's no envelope. Do you mean a wax seal?" Jazz asked.

"Yes."

"If Juliet knew how it worked," Jazz reasoned aloud. "Why would she open it? Unless, she had help."

"She didn't read it," Jenks said. "Not unless she could read whatever language that is. Beyond English and French, I'm lost. That hen scratching looks like Hindi, Chinese, hell, I don't know."

"So, she opened the seal." Jazz pointed her finger to mark off each step as she spoke them. "I presume there was a long enough delay that she could try to read it. It burst into flames, burning her fingers and she dropped it."

Jazz dropped to one knee to examine the floor. She ran her finger over the charred wood and motioned Jenks over.

"Feel the edge of that hole," she instructed him.

He felt the spot moving his finger in a circle as Jazz had done. He looked at her, shook his head and shrugged.

"The hole was not made from something burning through the wood. Not from this side. Something or someone pushed the edges up when it came into the room from below."

"*Now* you're creeping *me* out," Jenks said.

"Let's take a look downstairs and see what might have done it," Jazz said, standing to her feet.

Moments later the three of them stood looking up at the bookstore ceiling.

"Nothing," Jenks announced the finding. "That kind of blows that idea all to bits."

"Don't be so sure," Jazz cautioned.

"Can we get out of here now?" Claudette pleaded impatiently.

"I'll take you back to the café," Jenks volunteered. "I'll have to come back here and wrap up though."

"I'd rather not go back there," Claudette said.

"Why don't you go back to the hotel with me," Jazz offered. "You won't have to be alone, and you'll still be near the café."

"I can't," Claudette said. "I shouldn't have left Virgie and Bud there alone. I just had to see Juliet and now I'm regretting that decision. Besides, staying busy will keep my mind off things."

"Then let me go along and help for an hour or two," Jazz replied.

"Are you worried about me?" Claudette asked.

"Yes, as a matter of fact I am."

By the time they arrived back at the café, Jazz's apprehension had spread to the others. Jenks insisted on walking them inside and having a look around. Other than the elderly Virgie teetering on the brink of exhaustion, the café appeared as they left it.

"Lordy, Miz Claudette, am I glad to see you," Virgie greeted them without looking up from the order she was filling.

"I brought help," the owner replied passing behind Virgie and taking aprons from a nearby hook. "Jazz is going to help us out for a couple of hours."

"Lord knows we need it," Virgie said placing a box of beignets next to the register. "That'll be $19, ma'am."

With a smile, the woman handed Virgie a twenty.

"Oh please, keep the change. I love your little café," she said, pulling something from her purse. "Here's a little gift for the owner."

She placed a small parchment scroll on the counter, quickly turned and started through the crowd for the door.

"Miz Claudette, that lady wanted me to give you this," Virgie said holding out the scroll in her boss's direction.

Claudette screamed, threw her hands above her shoulders and backed away. Jazz stepped between Virgie and Claudette.

"Which lady?" she asked.

"Why, her, that one in the black cape." Virgie pointed at the woman in the doorway.

The woman looked back over her shoulder at Jazz, smiled and wriggled her fingers in a wave. Jazz dashed around the counter and shouldered patrons aside as she pushed through to the door. Clearing the door, she turned left along the sidewalk. It didn't take long to catch up to the cloak. A teenager picked it up from the ground and held it up to her body.

"Which way did the woman wearing that go?" Jazz demanded holding the teen by both arms.

The girl pointed the way and Jazz raced on in pursuit. She caught a glimpse of the woman she was after. The woman was wearing a gold and purple dress. She looked back, saw Jazz closing on her, and began shoving her way through the crowd.

Won't be hard to follow now.

Jazz had second thoughts when the woman caught hold of a wrought iron fence, leaped over it with ease, and ran down a narrow walkway between buildings. Jazz matched the move. She had more speed and tackled the fleeing woman. They rolled to a stop in a heap. The woman broke free, jumped to her feet, and turned on Jazz with burning red eyes and a savage growl. Jazz answered the challenge in kind.

Eyes locked the rougarous let the transformation become complete. A blast of breath caught Jazz's ear. Her foe slapped at her neck. The change back to human was quick, so too was the poison. The woman barely had time to form tears before she fell.

A shadow slipped behind the corner of the building at the end of the walkway. Jazz went after the killer who quickly ducked inside a silver Mercedes that sped off down Exchange Place scattering pedestrians who strayed off the sidewalk.

Ed's going to be thrilled.

CHAPTER 10

On his third try, Landry found the float to which he was assigned. The sight of all the men dressed as ridiculously as he was eased his mind even though it did nothing to ease Johnny's ribbing.

"Landry," a voice behind him called. "Where's your costume? No street clothes allowed."

"Very funny, Nelson," Landry replied turning to face his friend. "A gaudy jester is more your kind of look though."

"Yeah, you got no sense of humor—never did." Nelson pointed to a small group of Cupids passing by. "At least we're not wearing that get up. Good thing because you don't have the legs for it."

"I'll have you know, I have great legs," Landry teased. "But I still wouldn't be caught dead dressed like that."

"Where's your mask?"

Landry slid a corner of the mask from his shirt. "And that's where it's stay until we start to roll. So, what do we do now?"

"We guard the cooler over there," Nelson said with a toss of his head in the direction of a large orange cooler.

"You're kidding, right?"

"Nope, come on."

Nelson led him over to the cooler and removed the lid. It was filled with bottles of beer packed in ice.

"It does make sense to post a guard," Landry agreed, reaching for a bottle. "Some underage kids might stumble upon it."

“Right. We’re just doing our civic duty keeping the streets and our kids safe.”

“Semper fi.” Landry touched his bottle to Nelson’s, and they went in search of a place to sit, making sure to keep the cooler in sight. Their position and objective secured, they sipped their beer in a silence only old friends can share.

“Ready for reinforcements?” Nelson broke the silence.

He walked to the cooler and returned with two fresh beers.

“I heard you got married,” Nelson said. “About time, if you ask me. Where is she?”

“She said she was going shopping,” Landry said. “She’ll meet the parade when we get to St. Charles.”

“That sounds expensive.”

“Maybe,” Landry replied. “But she didn’t exactly say what she was going shopping for.”

“You worried there’s somebody else?” Nelson asked.

“Yes, but not like you think. We’re working a case.”

“Like that business with Jake awhile back?”

“How do you know about that?”

“Are you kidding? Everybody in the old squad knows. Seems Jake still can’t keep a secret. Bet he’s quit ribbing you about...well...you know.”

“Yeah, what about you?” Landry asked.

“I always believed you. Like that guy on Ghostbuster’s, I’ve seen some stuff that’ll turn you white.”

Landry wiped his fingers across Nelson’s cheek, then rubbed them together. “I think you’re exaggerating about that.”

“Only a little,” Nelson replied, and they both laughed.

“Maybe we should swap masks then,” Landry said.

“Done,” Nelson proposed, handing over his mask. “To hell with political correctness.”

“You got that right,” Landry replied as the exchange was completed.

Late that afternoon Landry and Nelson were relieved of cooler duty and took their places on the float moments before it began to move. The party atmosphere around the staging area at City Park opened onto miles packed with revelers. Landry and his buddy tossed strings of beads to the shouts and cheers of partygoers along the route.

“Hey, throw me some,” a buxom blonde shouted at Landry, punctuating the request by lifting her shirt.

“I told you it would be fun,” Nelson said with an elbow to Landry’s side.

“That’s trouble, not fun,” Landry told him.

“True, but worth a look.”

Dat’s rat. Lookin’ at dat get you in trouble. Good thing you got me to look for you, Johnny reminded him.

“Who’s Johnny?” Nelson asked.

“Johnny?”

“Yeah, you just said, ‘You’re supposed be watching me, Johnny’. So, who’s Johnny.”

“I did? Forget it, he’s nobody.”

Merci beaucoup to you too, Eddie, Johhny said. *I got half a mind not to tell you dere’s your wife.*

Landry hooted at Johnny attempt at humor until he realized they had reached St. Charles and Jazz was frantically waving to him. It was not “hello” she was signaling. Jenks was beside her.

Landry muttered a curse under his breath before turning to Nelson. “Got to go.”

Landry swung a leg over the rail and jumped from the moving float. He hit the ground, tucked and rolled. He came up on his feet still in one unbroken piece. Jenks and Jazz came running toward him. Jenks was pointing at something over Landry’s shoulder. Jazz broke off to her left against the tide of the parade.

Landry looked back to see what had the detective’s

attention. Nelson was slumped against the float with something protruding from him.

"Help Jazz. I got the guy on the float," Jenks shouted, chasing after the float.

Landry set off in the direction he saw Jazz going. He caught up to her a few blocks down the road. She was standing over a disheveled, bloody Cupid.

"What the hell is going on?" Landry asked.

"Let's get this guy in Jenks car and I'll tell you," she answered, hauling the battered Cupid off the pavement.

Landry caught the man by the arm and shoved him back in the direction from which they had just come. Jazz got a grip on the man's other arm that made him wince.

"You want to tell me now why you tried to kill my husband?" Jazz asked as they marched him along the street.

"He what?"

"He thought an arrow from his bow might help our love."

Landry wheeled around and delivered a right hook to Cupid's midsection that drove the little god's breath from him and made his knees buckle. Landry and Jazz kept him upright and got him moving again.

"If he dies, you're a dead man," Landry growled.

"Ow," Cupid said when they had gone only a few feet.

Before they could make it back to the spot where the chase began, Cupid went rigid before going into convulsions. They eased him to the ground as gently as the seizures would allow. A moment later, he was dead. The tiny hole in the back of his neck explained what happened.

"Poor sap," Landry said. "Couldn't have happened to a nicer guy."

Over the noise of the celebration, the first faint sound of sirens reached them.

"Those will be for your friend," Jazz said. "Stay with this guy. I'll go get Jenks to call this in. We have to talk."

"I hate it when you say that."

Jazz sniffed the air. "You've been drinking beer without me."

"It's Mardi Gras" Landry explained with a weak smile. "Better go get Jenks."

Landry finished up with Jenks's questions about Cupid about the time the media arrived, and the body was being hauled away. He and Jazz made their way to Tulane Medical center, dodged a television camera lurking in the Emergency Room entrance, and discovered Nelson had been sent to surgery. Navigating a maze of hallways and information desks, they found the Surgery waiting area.

"He's my brother," Landry said when asked if he was family.

It's not stretching the truth too much, he told himself.

"Let's talk over there," Jazz said pointing at the least crowded corner of the room.

"I suppose we have to," Landry conceded. "So much for Madri Gras."

"Next year, it's Mamou—maybe," Jazz replied.

"So, what did Cupid interrupt? It looked urgent," Landry said.

"After dropping you off, I went back to the café. Jenks was there. Seems he didn't know as much about his girlfriend as he thought. Anyway, while I was there, we got word Juliet was dead. It was a voodoo death curse, but it was delivered by something not exactly voodoo and not exactly of this world."

"That would be too easy," Landry said.

"Whatever Juliet saw literally scared her to death. When we got back to the café, another message was delivered to Claudette. She's okay," Jazz added when

Landry appeared ready to ask. "I chased after the woman who delivered it. I had her cornered, but she got a dart just like Cupid."

"So, whatever is going on it's well organized and multilayered."

"Exactly," Jazz replied. "And Marie is at the top. Claudette isn't just interested in moving up. She's been actively leading a local revolt."

"Who is here for Mr. Nelson?" the woman at the desk asked.

Landry was joined at the desk by a young woman in her twenties. She was dressed in extremely short shorts and a sleeveless, low-cut tee shirt that revealed more flawless skin than Landry care to think about at the moment.

"What relation are you to the patient?" the clerk asked.

"I'm his girl fr…er…fiancée," the young woman announced.

"And you, sir?" the woman behind the desk asked Landry.

"I'm…ah…I'm his." Landry shook his head trying to chase away the fiancée idea. "I'm his brother."

The young woman's head snapped in Landry's direction. Fire flared in her eyes, but she said nothing.

"Well, Mr. Nelson is in Recovery and stable. He will be going to Room 512. You both should go to the fifth floor waiting and they will let you know when he can have visitors."

"Why did you say he's your brother?" the young woman muttered when they stepped away from the desk.

Landry took her by the arm and pointed to Jazz. "That's my wife. Let's step over there and you can tell us why you claimed to be his fiancée."

She let Landry lead her. A few paces from Jazz the woman froze. She took a step back and Landry caught her arm.

"It's okay," he said, tugging her forward and taking a seat between them. "Jazz this is...what did you say your name was?"

"I didn't and don't plan to until you answer my question. Why did you say that you are Quinton's brother?"

"Quinton?" Landry asked. A light came over his clouded expression "Oh, yeah, I guess that is his name. He's always been Nelson to me. We served in Vietnam together, that makes us brothers. Now you."

"I didn't play with the truth, Mr. Landry," she replied. "*Quinton* really is my fiancé."

"You got to be kidding me, you're—"

A hand on Landry's arm stopped him. He looked at Jazz who smiled and slowly shook her head.

"What's your name?" Jazz asked. "And how do you know Marie Dupree?"

The woman could not hide the shock on her face at the mention of Marie.

"My name is Alice Scott. I suppose it will do no good to lie. I am Marie's...uh...follower."

"Ever used a dart blowgun?" Landry asked.

"No, never, why would I? Isn't that just in the jungle movies?"

"Afraid not," Jazz answered. "It seems your leader has developed a fondness for it. There are two of your fellow followers who could verify what I say, except, well, they're dead."

"Dart in the neck," Landry added, tapping the back of his neck. "Nasty stuff."

"Does Quinton know about your involvement with Marie?" Jazz asked.

"He's a Vodouisant," Alice answered.

"Is that a yes or a no?" Jazz pressed her.

"He worships Bondye and does not care what Marie does."

"That's better," Jazz assured her. "Then, we can probably assume the arrow was meant for Landry."

"Arrow? What arrow? The police told me he was in an accident, fell off the float or something like that."

"Something like that," Landry said.

CHAPTER 11

Landry reached around Alice to push open the door to Room 512 for her. She spent a silent moment taking in the scene before breaking into a run for Nelson's bed.

"Quint," she squealed, throwing herself on him and smothering him with kisses.

Nelson winced with pain and slowly pushed her away. "I love you, but, ah, well..."

He pointed to the tube running from his chest to a contraption on the floor beside the bed. The water in the plastic device moved in time to his breathing.

"Oh my God, what have they done to you?" Alice moaned, backing away.

"You don't need to be that far away. *And* my lips aren't injured," Nelson said.

She came to him with halting steps and trembling hands to peck him on the lips. He pulled her to him and applied a long lingering kiss that was more to his liking.

"I'm not gonna break. I'm sore not fragile," he told her and pointed toward the door. "Who are these folks you brought along?"

"Nelson," Landry said stepping up to shake his friend's hand. "I'm not sure I like your idea of a good time at Mardi Gras."

"Ain't that the truth," Nelson replied. "But I've seen your ugly mug before I was asking about the lovely lady over there."

Landry held out a hand and Jazz stepped over to take it. "This is my wife, Jasmine. She has to like you before you can call her Jazz. In your case, that's not likely to happen. I mean, hell, I don't even like you."

"Don't listen to him. Call me Jazz," she said reaching out to shake Nelson's hand.

"Jazz, I'm not sure you really like me. I take an arrow in the lung and all I get is a handshake?"

Jazz leaned over to kiss Nelson on the cheek. "Better?"

"Better. How a gruesome dude like Landry, with the personality of a rock, ended up married to a beauty like you, has got to be one of the great mysteries of the universe."

"I like you better already," Jazz said. "He's just an incredibly lucky guy. Looks like you are two of a kind."

"Semper fi," they said together.

"Listen, would you ladies mind if Landry and I talked in private for a few minutes?"

"Man talk? Really Quinton that so chauvinist," Alice said.

"Marine talk," Nelson countered.

"You can't fight that," Jazz told her. "Let's go get something to drink."

"That's some voodoo doll you have there, old buddy," Landry said. "I didn't know you were into voodoo."

"I wasn't. I didn't say anything back then but in Nam I saw that thing you did. After the ribbing you took, there was no way I was going to say anything."

"I can't blame you there. What's that got to do with voodoo?

"I did tell people after we got back to the world. Big mistake except for the Indians I met, and the voodoo community. They believed. They made me feel at home."

Landry nodded remembering how hard it was to fit in after the war.

"You're something of a celebrity in New Orleans voodoo. Infamous might be a better word after what you did to Mama Lille.

"I didn't do anything to Mama Lille, but almost die. She disappeared. Honestly, I don't know more than that."

"Marie Dupree doesn't believe that," Nelson said. "She thinks you killed her Daddy too."

"Ah, I am guilty of that one," Landry replied. "You know I've never come right out and told that to anyone but Jazz."

"It's not a secret. You're not after me, are you? I mean the arrow and all."

"No, should I be? Have you done something to make an old friend try and kill you?"

"I'm a Vodouisant."

"So?

"So, isn't that what you do—eliminate vodouisants?"

"Only the ones who are trying to kill me. Although, I have been known to kill a rougarou or two who were terrorizing their towns. Mostly I try to mind my own business and fail badly at it. It's cold comfort but the arrow was probably meant for me courtesy of Marie Dupree."

"So now we're square?" Nelson asked.

"Yeah, I'd say so. If you're counting those things. Now, what's going on that Alice and her friends want me dead?"

"Alice doesn't—"

Landry held up a hand to cut him off. "I got the impression that Alice is tight with Marie even if you're not. Am I wrong?"

"No, you're not wrong. But I can't believe she would do anything like this."

"Did she ask you to get me on the float?"

Nelson studied Landry's face, met his eyes, and held them long enough for Landry to deduce the answer.

"Yes," Nelson finally whispered.

Landry gave him a slow nod. "Forget it. You didn't know."

"How can you say that?" Nelson asked.

"I don't know how. I know you. I just know you weren't involved."

"What do we do now?"

"We? Look, buddy, there's no we—not this time. You stay out of this. Stay away from Alice, stay away from Marie. In fact, stay away from everything in this city connected in any way with voodoo."

"Promise me you won't hurt Alice," Nelson pleaded.

"I'll do my best," Landry promised. "I'm giving her the same advice, but it's up to her."

Landry held the door open for a somewhat less enthusiastic Alice. He took a long look back at his friend and closed the door.

"Everything okay in there?" Jazz asked when he moved away from Nelson's room.

"I think so."

"Good because we need to talk." Jazz smiled at the pained look on Landry's face following her announcement.

"Is it bad?" he asked.

"It's complicated."

Landry threw up his hands. "Of course it is, wouldn't have it any other way. But take me someplace where they serve beer to tell me."

"I think that would be wise," Jazz agreed.

Back out on the street they decided walking might be the fastest and easiest mode of travel. They started out moving south along the crowded streets weaving through groups of drunken revelers, bouncing off people walking in the opposite direction, and fighting off the feeling that they were exposed. They made a left turn, headed east and the crowds seemed to double.

"Do we know where we're going?" Landry asked.

"Yeah, that Irish pub near the hotel."

"One of the many reasons I love you."

"What, you love because I buy you that awful beer you drink?" Jazz asked with a smile.

"Kind of, I love you because you know me and still love me."

They arrived at the Kerry a short time later. Landry pushed his way to the door, peered inside, and shook his head. The dimly lit, narrow pub was packed shoulder to shoulder with patrons.

"I don't think so," Landry said.

"Let me see," Jazz replied stepping around him. "Oh, there's a little table by the pool table. Wait here a minute while I go claim it."

Landry watched her shapely figure navigate through the bar.

She's beautiful, but she's blind. That table's not empty.

Dat's what you think, Johnny told him. *Folks make room for a lady like dat.*

Wanna bet?

Sure, but you ain't got nothing ol' St. Pierre wants. Regardez.

Jazz reached the table and leaned in close to the women seated at the table. Landry imagined her smile disappearing as they refused to vacate. To his surprise the women jumped from their seats and rushed past Jazz for the door without stopping to pay. A bar man shouted at them and started around the bar. Jazz intercepted him and after a word from her, he returned to his duties. Jazz waved Landry in while she claimed one of the chairs at the empty table.

Told you so, Johnny said and laughed. *O ye of da little faith.*

Landry wound his way through the bar to sit opposite Jazz.

"Do I want to know what you said to them?" he asked.

"I don't know, do you? I just offered to let you pay

their tab."

"And?"

"Well, maybe just one little growl and a toothy smile."

CHAPTER 12

Landry took a big gulp of his beer, sighed and tried to smile.

"Okay, I'm ready," he said squaring his shoulders. "Fire away. What did you learn from Alice?"

"After I opened the conversation," Jazz began, pausing just long enough to flash him a smile. "She decided it was in her best interest to tell me something. I'm sure *some* of it was true."

"I guess that's the best we can hope for."

"True and what wasn't the truth probably was more supposition than outright lies. She seemed a little frightened."

"You think?"

"Not of me," Jazz said laying an innocent hand over her heart. "Okay, maybe a little of me, but she knew what I was when we met. You saw her shrink away. Marie is purging those she thinks aren't in with her a hundred percent. She killed Juliet and took a shot at Claudette, Alice is friends with them, but not part of their rebellion. She's solidly with Marie, but the others have been trying to woo her away."

"She's important to whatever is going on then?"

"If Marie had an inner circle, young Alice would be one of them," Jazz answered. "At least, that's my feeling."

"But Marie's too paranoid to actually have an inner circle," Landry said.

"Exactly. Evidently Cupid was a good shot. His orders were to only wound you, so he wasn't aiming for center body mass. You upset the plan, and his aim, by jumping off the float when you did. Nelson is collateral damage."

"If Alice was in on that plan, Marie might believe his wounding has driven Alice to the other side," Landry speculated.

"*That's* why she's scared."

"Any chance we can use that to our advantage?" Landry asked.

"There's always a chance, but it's not likely. The good news is that Marie is leaving New Orleans tonight. The bad news is, that probably means she's already given orders for while she's gone. There's something big going down and that damned book is at the heart of it."

"I take it Marie, Clemenceau, and our missing jaguar aren't through."

"He goes by Wilson now, but you're right," Jazz said. "He's made new friends in Salem. As you might imagine, *that* has made Marie nervous. So nervous in fact that she's willing to sic us on her partner."

"Then, she'll knock off the battered winners and claim the spoils for herself. She has a lot of confidence in us."

"The enemy of my enemy..." Jazz said with a shrug. "She won't come right out and help us, but she will grease the skids and work behind the scenes when it's to her advantage."

"So, we are off to Salem?" Landry asked.

"On the next flight we can find. I'll put Miz Clara on it."

"In that case, I'd better finish this beer in a hurry."

***

Delta Flight 765 touched down at Boston Logan International mid-morning on Wednesday. Landry had found time for a few more beers, a shower, and a change of clothes the night before. He and Jazz spent their time in the air snoozing with their heads together. One of the flight attendants commented that they made a romantic sight. Landry found it more of a pain in the neck.

"You're getting old, you cradle robber," Jazz teased.

"Getting old is a habit I hope to continue," Landry replied.

Just beyond the gate, a man with steel gray hair in a black suit caught Landry's eye. It was the sign he held more than the man himself that was worthy of attention. LANDRY the sign proclaimed in large block letters.

"A limo, really?" Landry said. "She's truly gone overboard this time."

"I don't think so," Jazz told him taking him by the arm and pulling him along.

"Mister and missus Landry?" the man asked as they approached.

"Guilty," Landry said.

"Sorry about the sign. Clara's description was right on, but I was afraid you might miss me. I'm Sam Killebrew. I am...*was*...a friend of Father Paul."

"Hello, Sam," Jazz greeted him with an outstretched hand. "Please call me Jazz. This is my husband Ed...er...better make that Landry."

"Ex-military, and never really get used to using the first name, got it."

"Clara thought it best to bypass the rental car," Sam said, producing a set of keys from his pocket. "I have one of mine in the lot. I'll take you to it and then get a cab home. But, first, your bags. This way."

"Did Father Paul leave anything in your car when he left? A book, maybe?" Landry asked.

"I didn't see anything out of the ordinary but help yourself. There's a key to Father's office on that ring. I have his books and private papers at my house. You're welcome to stay with me while you're in town."

"That might be dangerous," Landry warned.

"I know that vengeance belongs to the Lord," Sam said. "But I'm ready to do what I can to get back at the people who killed Father Paul."

"And we try never to turn down help," Jazz replied. "We'd love to stay with you."

"Great. I'll get that cab. I think you two should go check out the church and his office before we talk. Here's my address and my phone number along with the address for the church."

"Thanks, Miz Clara told us how to get to the church," Jazz said. "She seems to share your opinion that it should be our first stop."

"We'll call you when we are on our way to your place," Landry added.

"God be with you, Sam replied before walking away.

Jazz shivered the moment they stepped inside the church. It was not caused by the northern winter chill. She laid a hand on Landry's arm holding him just inside the door. He gave her a quizzical look but said nothing. They remained where they were trying to put a name to the feeling. There was an underlying sense of being watched. The empty nave was quiet. That was to be expected on a weekday morning. The sense that they were not alone was unsettling.

"What is it?" Landry whispered.

"I'm not sure."

"It reminds me of someone glaring at me."

Jazz slowly nodded agreement. The feeling was a kind of disembodied anger. It was not directed *at* them. It just seemed to occupy the room.

"Let's go sit a minute," she said.

Their footsteps echoed as they walked down the aisle of the sanctuary. They settled into a pew about halfway to the altar. They had not been there long when a door closed somewhere behind them, and footsteps approached. Landry looked over his shoulder and was relieved to see a dark-haired man with a fleck of gray above his right eye that made him look as if he encountered an errant paint brush. He was in late thirties, wearing a charcoal gray suit and shirt notched with a clerical collar. He made the sign of the cross as he turned down the aisle toward them. He smiled as he drew near, and the feeling of an angry watcher faded. When the man stopped at their pew, the feeling vanished altogether.

"I am Deacon Kevin McBride," he introduced himself.

"Ed Landry. This is my wife, Jasmine."

"Please to meet you. Deacon Sam told me you were coming today. How may I help you?"

"*Deacon* Sam, is it?" Landry said. "He forgot to mention that."

"Sam, that is, Deacon Sam," Jazz added. "Said we might have a look in Father Paul's office. It *is* still unoccupied, isn't it?"

"Father Paul's replacement has not yet arrived," the Deacon replied, and his smile vanished. "I will let you decide if his office is unoccupied."

"This just keeps getting better," Landry mumbled.

"Pardon me?" the deacon replied.

Jazz gave Landry's biceps a sharp punch. "Pay no attention to him. His grumbling just means his caffeine level is low."

"I may be able to help with that. Follow me."

They followed the deacon to an office. Desks sat along the walls to either side of the door. A table with a printer, and a makeshift coffee bar sat beneath the window in the far wall. The deacon picked up a decanter holding three fingers of pitch-black liquid and started to dump it down the small sink.

"Don't throw that away," Landry said a sense of urgency in his voice.

The deacon stopped with the pot canted at forty-five degrees above the sink. "It will only take a few minutes to make a pot."

"No need," Landry told him. "There's nothing like coffee aged all morning in a church pot. That ink black stuff looks just about right."

"Really, it's no trouble."

"Landry wouldn't lie—in church anyway," Jazz said with a laugh. "He'll drink that *and* actually enjoy it."

The deacon poured the coffee into a cup and handed it to Landry before making the sign of the cross. Landry took a sip, smiled and proclaimed it as good as the wine in Cana.

"What *are* we going to find in the Father Paul's old office?" Jazz asked while Landry continued to sip.

"I don't know," Deacon Kevin answered. "That's not a dodge. There is something there. Are you familiar with the Book of Enoch and the concept of Watchers?"

"Vaguely," Jazz replied.

"Whatever is in that office has to be something supernatural. Though the Church might not agree to anything supernatural whether Watcher, spirit, specter, or *witch*."

The slight upward inflection on the last word sounded to Landry like the deacon was sounding them out.

"I hear Father Paul was interested in witches," Landry replied. "Are you a believer in such things?"

"You can't believe the Bible and not believe witches exist, Deacon Kevin said.

"It may sound like a strange question," Jazz prefaced her question. "But do *you*, that is you personally, believe the Bible?"

"Yes, yes, I do. Which means I do believe in witches. Although, I think this thing we are talking about is not a witch, but something stronger. That said, I'll wait here for you to return. Maybe you can tell me."

Landry leaned against one of the desks studying their host while he finished his coffee. The cop in

Landry told him that the man was hiding something. He wasn't being untruthful. He just wasn't telling them the whole story. Whatever he was holding back, it was fear, uncertainty or both, not duplicity gripping him.

"Okay," Landry said putting down his cup. "Let's investigate."

"That's why we're here," Jazz replied rising from her seat.

"Father Paul's office is two doors down on the right," Deacon Kevin told them. "I'll wait here, if it's all the same to you."

"No problem," Landry assured him with a thumbs up and closed the door behind them.

Deacon Kevin crossed himself and began to pray.

CHAPTER 13

Landry leaned a shoulder against the doorframe outside the priest's office and rapped gently. Jazz gave him a "what-the-heck-are-you-doing" look as he paused as if waiting for an answer. He smiled at her and opened the door.

"No sense being impolite," he quipped.

Dim light filtered in through the stained-glass window to paint the desk and the wall behind it with long red roses. Landry found the switch and flipped on the half dozen wall sconces around the room. The walls were covered with dark oak paneling that lent to the dark feel of the room. On the wall behind the desk to Landry's left, shelves of books reached to the ceiling. A rolling ladder stationed near the far side of the shelves provided access to the top. Except for the area around the desk and the books, the room was covered in a thick navy-blue carpet. In front of the desk sat a pair of King Louis chairs upholstered in blue leather that matched the color of the office chair behind it.

"Rather somber, isn't it?" Landry asked.

Jazz put a finger to her lips and shook her head. He nodded understanding and reached over to pull the door closed behind them. Turning back, a glance at Jazz sent a chill through him. Her lips and nose were twitching with a canine prelude to baring teeth in a growl. Her hands were clenched into white knuckled fists. Then, she did growl. It was a warning that rumbled low in her throat.

Landry reached for her. She slapped his hand away before dropping to the floor and beginning to seize. He knelt beside her trying to protect her head that was beating out a staccato rhythm on the carpet. A sudden gust of wind and the fluttering of pages carried to him the unmistakable feeling of another presence. Landry slowly rose to his full height and turned to face the threat. That it was a threat seemed certain from the moment he felt it.

A little slow on the upchuck there, Eddie, Johnny chided him.

Landry ignored him, focusing on the shapeless mist occupying the priest's chair. He said nothing, content for the moment to plant his hands on his hips and wait. The grunts and growls coming from the floor behind him faded to a stop. He could hear Jazz breathing heavily and resisted the urge to go to her. He was determined not to show weakness. Let whatever it was think he didn't care. That would be its first mistake.

The mist was coalescing into the form of a woman with dark hair.

Wait for it, Landry, he told himself. *Let it throw the first punch.*

Dat be foolish rat dere, Johhny warned.

Jazz brushed his elbow as she moved to his side. He refused to take his eyes from the woman in the chair. The face formed completely, and her body became a black dress below a large white collar.

Hey dere, pilgrim, Johnny did a poor imitation of John Wayne.

Landry couldn't help but smile. The crack of happiness in Landry's stoney face stirred the specter into action. The thing leaped up from the chair and pointed a hooked finger at Jazz.

"Witch! She's a witch," the specter shouted and began to laugh.

"You're no ghost," Jazz said.

"That's because I'm not really here. *And* I'm not a witch, they don't exist. You're just making it up to spread fear." The specter began to laugh once more.

"What's so funny," Landry asked. "What you did to Father Paul was no joke."

"Prove it," the woman challenged him. "Surely, you've noticed that witches are hard to put on trial these days. It's kept religious fanatics like you at bay for three hundred years now."

"We don't try witches, vampires, or—" Jazz began.

"Or rougarous?" the specter finished for her.

"Or rougarous," Jazz affirmed with a nod of her head."

"Yeah, trials are so costly and messy," Landry added.

"Little man, what makes you think you shall succeed where the priest failed?"

"Unlike the Father, I'm not interested in forgiveness, or salvation," Landry told the fading mist. "I'm more of an exterminator. I won't hesitate."

The mist vanished entirely leaving Jazz and Landry in the not quite empty room.

"It's not gone, is it?" Landry asked.

"Whatever we were talking to is gone," Jazz said. "The thing that lives here is still around."

"And what might that be?"

"Let's find out," Jazz told him and whirled around to face the empty room. "You want to show your real face, now? If you're shy, you could just tell us your name."

The response to Jazz's taunting was not quantifiable in a tangible way. It was more the sense of something huge pressing itself into the room. As it grew, so did the sensation of being touched by something slimy, wet, and hairy.

Like snuggling up to a nutria rat, Landry thought as beside him, Jazz gagged. *Yeah, sort of like that.*

Seemingly without thought, their hands found each other, their fingers intertwined, and they drew themselves up a little taller. Defiant silence met the unseen presence slithering over them. The sound of someone or something drawing in a deep breath was accompanied by the arrival of an icy chill that raised gooseflesh on their arms. Landry clenched his jaws to keep his teeth from chattering in the cold and exhaled misty plumes. He and Jazz exchanged glances. Neither showed signs of fear or retreat.

Hot, humid air rushed into the room. Behind it, words came at last. They were spoken in the soft confidential tones of the confessional, but there was nothing holy in the voice that dripped venom.

"You are strong, but a glimpse of my real face would drive you insane," it said. "What's in a name? I have many. Most of which you could not pronounce."

"Try us," Jazz said.

"Oh, I have," the voice replied. "That is, I have begun to. I accept the challenge, though the end is not in question."

"We might surprise you," Landry said.

Maniacal laughter filled the room. The image flashed in Landry's of a head thrown back and rows of needle-like teeth guarding the entrance to the sound. When the laughter faded away, the voice was back.

"That would be amusing. I have not been surprised by men in millennia. Perhaps we will talk again. However, before I entertain your pleas for mercy—the trial you asked for."

The thing receded in a swirling gust of wind leaving the air with a stale taste. Jazz went to search the priest's desk while Landry returned to the books. He pulled two from their places and sat to flip through the pages.

"Are you checking those from the late Father's library or planning to read them here?" Jazz asked, satisfied the desk held no secrets.

"That depends on how strict the deacon's check out policy is," he answered.

"So, you'll steal them if you have to?"

"Borrow, Jazz dear, borrow."

"Right. Let's go."

Jazz opened the door, gasped, and took a step back.

"Sorry, I didn't mean to startle you," said a tall, raven-haired man in a gray suit. "I'm Deacon Wayne. I was just coming to check on you."

The deacon's stern angular face, stoney expression, and flat voice lacked the sorrow his words offered. His deep-set dark eyes were equally devoid of warmth. Jazz flashed him a quick smile.

"As you can see, we're fine," she said. "Is Deacon Kevin still in his office?"

"Yes, he's still in *our* office, Wayne replied. "I really need to hurry on. Can you find your way alone?"

He turned and hustled away without waiting for a reply. Jazz looked at Landry who responded with a smile and a shrug of his shoulders.

"How long do you think he had been standing there?" Jazz asked.

"Oh, probably since the moment he found out we were in there."

"That would be my guess too," she told him. "Why not just wait with Kevin? We said we'd come back and tell him what we thought."

"I'd say they both knew what we would find," Landry said. "Kevin didn't want any part of it, but Wayne—"

"Was rooting for the other team," Jazz finished for him.

Landry motioned for Jazz to enter the office and followed her inside. Kevin stood and came around his desk to meet them.

"Can I get you another cup of coffee, Mr. Landry?" he asked.

"Just Landry will do. I'm not in the habit of turning down coffee, but I don't need it, if that's what you're getting at."

"I have a feeling I will need some. Ma'am how about you?"

"It sounds like the sociable thing to do. Yes, I'd love some, thank you," Jazz replied.

When coffee was served and everyone seated, the deacon looked at them over the rim of his cup and smiled.

"Well?" he asked.

"The room is definitely still occupied," Landry answered.

"I suppose that's makes it a kind of good news-bad news situation," Kevin said. "The good news is, it's not my imagination. The bad news also is, it's not my imagination. My question for you two is, what is it?"

"Before we venture a guess, how about you answer some questions for us?" Jazz asked.

"If I can. Fire away."

"When did the presence we felt in there show up?"

"I'm going to assume you felt the same slimy, rotten evil thing I did," Kevin began. "I felt a strange sort of uneasiness in Father's office about a month, maybe six weeks, before he vanished. But nothing on the scale of what I felt two days ago. I haven't been in there since."

"Do you know if Sam felt it?"

"He hasn't said anything," Kevin replied. "But he hasn't been his usual self since Father's been gone."

"What about Deacon Wayne?" Landry asked.

"Who?"

"Deacon Wayne. Thirtyish, about 6'3", 200 pounds, pasty complexion, no personality."

Kevin shook his head. "There's no deacon here like that. Just Sam, me and Michael, who is away on a sabbatical."

He walked over to the neighboring desk and handed Landry a framed photograph of a man in his forties, crew cut sandy hair. Unless the woman and teenaged girls next to him were taller than most women, Michael was under six feet tall.

"Has there ever been a deacon named Wayne here?" Jazz asked.

"Not that I know of," Kevin answered. A quick uplift of his head seemed to say an idea had come to him. "There are pictures in the parish archives dating back to the 1770s."

Landry looked at Jazz. "Might be worth a look," he said.

"Maybe, but not right now," Jazz said. "Right now, I think we take in some sights and head for Deacon Sam's place."

"Okay, if you say so," Landry agreed.

"Before you go," the deacon said. "What *is* in that room?"

"I'm not sure exactly," Jazz said. "It might be a book collector. I think we met not long ago."

CHAPTER 14

Jazz climbed into the car after their first stop, folded her arms across her chest, and fixed Landry with a mock scowl.

"I see how it is," Jazz said. "I take you to Mardi Gras. You throw me in a dungeon."

"You make it look good," Landry countered with a wry smile.

"Yeah, well, I hope lunch is included in this tour."

"That's our next stop. And here we are," Landry announced pulling into a spot off Derby Street near the Congress Street Bridge.

"Haven't you had enough witches yet?"

"I have but, unfortunately, I get the feeling that somehow we're just getting started."

They gave the sidewalk tables a forlorn glance and stepped inside the warmth of a spacious tavern. When a server arrived, they ordered clam chowder and fish and chips. Landry asked for the darkest beer they had. A groan of disappointment and a snicker from Jazz greeted the brew placed before him.

"The food looks good though," Jazz said with a tilt of her head toward a neighboring table. "But I think it's more than the beer that has you in a bummed fog."

"You're right about that. I'm missing something important, something that goes to the core of why we're here and Father Paul's death."

"Maybe the books you...ah...borrowed from his office will help."

"Maybe. I was hoping the re-enactment at the museum would jar it loose. It's like Poe's *The Purloined*

Letter. It's hiding in plain sight just daring people to see."

"And Father Paul was detective enough to see it," Jazz added.

"Yes, but that doesn't get us any closer to finding it."

"Excuse me," said a man at the next table. "Your accent drew me into a bit of innocent eavesdropping. In the process, I couldn't help but hear what you were talking about.

"Accent? What accent is dat y'all talkin' 'bout?" Landry asked in his best Cajun voice and followed it with a laugh.

"That would be the one," the man replied joining them in a laugh. "My name's Harris Goode. I'm the pastor at the Salem Church of God. I know...knew...Brother Paul. I still can't believe he's gone. Would it be okay if I join you?"

Landry looked at Jazz who nodded approval and held out a hand toward an empty chair across from them. "Please do, Reverend."

The preacher, dressed in a blue dress shirt open at the collar and black slacks stood with some effort. He gathered his coat and cane from the back of his chair and stepped over to their table. His sandy-red hair in a flattop cut, weathered face and limp prompted a question from Landry.

"Souvenir from the war?" he asked pointing at the cane.

"Yeah, '68 Chu Lai. You?"

Landry stood and shook Goode's hand. "'70 A Shau Valley." This is my wife, Jazz."

"A pleasure to meet you both," Goode said, shaking Jazz's hand.

"So, you knew Father Paul?" Jazz asked.

Goode held up his index finger, looked up and smiled at the server who had appeared.

"Would you like to order, sir?" the woman asked.

"Put it on my tab," Landry injected before his guest could speak. "I insist."

"Make it a Reuben and coffee then," Goode answered.

"Pardon me," Goode said when the server was gone. "Father Paul is well known around town, and not particularly well liked in some circles. I'm sure he still has enemies willing to slander his name. How do you know him?"

"He died in our hotel room in New Orleans on Sunday night," Jazz replied. "That was the first time we ever laid eyes on him. Just what was he up to here that made someone want him dead?"

"May I tell you a story to explain?"

"Absolutely," Landry agreed. "But let's wait on lunch so we're not interrupted."

After their food arrived and drinks were refilled, Goode began. His voice was clear and strong in keeping with his profession.

"I first met Father Paul about a year ago," Goode's voice cracked with his mention of the priest and paused to collect himself. "Sorry, he was a good man."

"We understand," Jazz told him.

"I had been at my church a short time, Goode continued. "A man in my congregation came to my office one afternoon. He was concerned because his daughter was not sleeping at night. She insisted on sleeping with her parents a few times. When asked why, she said a ghost woman come out of her closet at night.

"She had developed tremors that came and went during the day. These were coupled with periods of a kind of waking blackout. They took her to a doctor who diagnosed her with absence seizures and scheduled her to be tested further.

"Not completely satisfied with that explanation, the man set up a video monitor in the child's room. He brought me a recording that sent a chill through me. It showed the little girl talking with someone. The entire room was visible on the video. No one was there and no other voice heard though the girl was clearly answering questions. Near the end, the girl turned to look into the camera and hissed like a cat. The screen went black after that, but the look of evil in that child's eyes just before that happened will be with me forever.

"I went to the house. There was something that I can only describe as a presence there. I prayed room by room prayers of cleansing and protection over the house and the family. When it was over we all seemed to feel better. The video monitor stayed and there were no more conversations and no reports of ghosts from the girl."

"What does that have to do with Father Paul?" Jazz asked.

"About a week later, not far from where we are sitting, the girl and her father passed a woman on the street. The girl pointed at the woman swearing she was the lady from the closet. The woman stopped stared at the father and hissed at him before walking away. The family moved away two weeks later."

"I still don't get the connection," Landry said.

"Father Paul found out about the whole thing. I can't say for sure, but I think the family went to him after the incident on the street. He was doing research on the witch trials. He came to discuss the matter with me. He pointed out the similarity between what the family experienced and what happened in 1692 in Salem Village."

"And?" Jazz asked.

"He was right," Goode answered. "You haven't read his book, have you?"

"No, but I have it."

"Read it. Pay particular attention to what ended the trials."

"They were a sham, brought on by jealousy," Landry said.

"Were they?" Goode paused, his brow furrowed, and he looked at Landry. "And the rougarou, did I say that right, is that just a myth? You're not a man to dismiss things easily, Mr. Landry. Follow the money, that's what you lawmen say, isn't it?"

"Yeah, so?"

"So, look around you," Goode said. "What's *the* industry driving the economy here?

"I'd say tourism."

"And you'd be correct. Tourism built on the witch trials and the notion that they were either superstitious hysteria, toxin induced hallucination, or class rivalry, all turning on *the innocence of the accused.* What if the trials began with the truth and were hijacked by the guilty to serve as an unbreakable cover for their later activity?"

"Real witches?"

"Sort of the antithesis of New Orleans voodoo. You believe in that, don't you," Goode said rising to go.

"Wait," Jazz said. "How is it that you just happened to sit next to us?"

"The Lord works in mysterious ways. Here's my card if you should need me."

Goode passed Landry the card and started walking swiftly.

"Goode, wait, I have a question for you," Landry called after him.

The preacher kept walking as if he didn't hear.

CHAPTER 15

Landry shook his head as they watched the preacher leave the tavern. His curiosity was stirred more by the how and why of the encounter than the man himself. The clergyman himself was real enough. Jazz stowed Rev. Goode's card in her purse and gave Landry an odd, tilted head look.

"What?" she asked.

"Curiouser and curiouser," he replied. "That little visit has made me wonder about something, but let's save it for Deacon Sam's place later. We have places to go and things to see."

"Such as?"

"The Salem Witch Village, and the Witch Trials Memorial."

"Not my idea of fun, but then, we are working. If memory serves all of those places are an easy walk from here," Jazz said.

"Your memory is right on," Landry told her. "It's your willingness to brave the cold I'm wondering about."

"I can take it if you can.

Landry paid the check, and they stepped out into the chilly wind blowing in off the water. The walk was only a few blocks, and they set a brisk pace in an effort to keep warm.

The Witch Museum, inside an old gothic style church, had been less about artifacts than wax figure dioramas and audio explanations. On their way to the village, they skipped a stop at a museum that housed collection of witch boards.

"Nothing there we don't already kno—" Jazz's words were cut short.

Her head snapped sharply toward the far end of the building. She took a few jogging steps to get to the corner of the building and peered down the street.

"What is it?" Landry asked.

"I thought I saw a familiar face." Jazz waved for him to follow and started down the block.

At the next corner, they came to a brick walkway lined with small trees and shrubs that ran between the buildings.

"Follow the yellow…er…red brick road? Landry asked.

"It's going our way, why not?" Jazz answered.

"So, whose familiar face did you see?"

"I could swear it was Marie Dupree."

"If it was Marie, she's involved with someplace in the area," Landry said. "If we were being followed, she wouldn't be the one to do it."

"I say we get back to the tavern, warm up with some coffee," Landry suggested when they'd gone only a few blocks.

"My thoughts exactly," Jazz replied.

Back at the tavern and warmed by steaming cups of coffee, Jazz leaned back in her seat to study Landry's face.

"It doesn't look like our little walk did much in the way of moving us closer to your missing piece of the puzzle."

"On the contrary," Landry said. "Did you pick up the thread that runs through this entire town?"

"Witches. So what? It's Salem, that should be no surprise."

"Wrong. Witches is not the real common thread."

"Okay, I'm trying to channel your Poe idea," Jazz said, frowning and furrowing her brow in thought. "I give up."

"It seems important for every museum, shop, and landmark to tell everyone that they were not *really* witches at all. The common thread is that they were all falsely accused and irrefutably innocent of witchcraft. It is *imperative* to the narrative that every tourist take away that message *because* witches don't exist."

"And anyone who says otherwise is on a witch hunt," Jazz picked up his thought.

"The aggressive, deliberate, slander and false persecution of one's personal enemies," Landry added.

"Which forces people to accept modern witches as just a harmless earth-based religion."

"Like voodoo," Landry said. "And we both know how harmless that can be, don't we?"

"Except New Orleans voodoo is accepted as real even by those who don't truly believe in it. This cannot even be questioned as anything more than Puritan hysteria and blind persecution."

"It's the perfect defense. That's why I couldn't bring Johnny to trial."

"Because no one would believe it. Rougarous aren't real."

"Exactly. And if they were, there's no..." Landry's voice faded into thought before spring into life. "Evidence. The evidence, that's it."

"That's what?"

"The evidence, Jazz. They brought the witches to trial because they had *evidence*.

Jazz's eyes lit up as she caught where his thinking was going. Landry leaned over and kissed her.

"And the evidence was thrown out by—" She stopped and tilted her head. "By churchmen whose God rose from the dead and yet they shy away from the supernatural. Men like Cotton Mather."

"Mather was never involved in the trials though he did defend them. But he opposed the use of spectral evidence. That is what brought the trials to an end."

"No evidence, no more trials," Jazz said.

"Can you image what it would be like today to try and charge someone with a crime and have the word "witchcraft" come up?"

"No prosecutor would touch it," she assured him.

"No, but a priest might."

"We need more insight into Father Paul. Deacon Sam?" Jazz asked.

"Deacon Sam. Let's go."

Landry paid the bill and held the door for Jazz as they left the tavern. They walked around the corner of the building into the parking lot where they had left Sam's car. There was a pop that startled Landry. A young man suddenly stood up next to the car, a knife in his hand. He took a quick look at Landry and Jazz before running around the back of the car and down the lot.

"I got this," Jazz said going after him.

Landry walked over to inspect the damage. The driver's rear tire had a slit in the tire wall. Landry didn't stoop to inspect the damage; there was no need. There was, however, an interesting looking note on the windshield. He plucked the note from under the wiper blade and held it up.

Coonass Go Home

"Coonass? Who's that punk calling a coonass?"

Look like he got hisself caught by de rougarou, Johnny said. *Who da fool now?*

A sheepish looking kid of no more than nineteen approached on tip toe beside Jazz. She had a handful of the waist of his jeans that she held higher in the air than was comfortable.

I'll bet he hasn't worn his pants that high in years, Landry thought.

Dat's one fine woman you got dere, Johnny replied.

You got that right.

"Honey did you...ah?" Landry said.

"No," Jazz replied shaking her head. "Didn't need to, he's slow. You want me to introduce him to a new danger involved in vandalism?"

"Not yet."

"What are you two talking about? I didn't do nothin'," the youth maintained.

"Trust me," Landry said prodding the man's chest. "You don't want to know. That woman can chew you up and spit you out."

"She don't look so tough to me," he said, trying to jerk away.

Jazz lifted him off the ground, letting his crotch bear the bulk of his weight.

"Okay, okay, put me down" he pleaded.

Jazz lowered the youth enough to allow his feet to touch the ground.

"He had this," she said handing Landry the knife.

Landry held the knife under the young man's nose. "You ever see the movie Chinatown?"

Fear filled the youth's eyes, and he gave his head a fast shake.

"Figures," Landry said. "Now, you can remain all in one piece by simply telling us who put you up to this little stunt."

"Nobody I—"

"Stop right there," Landry commanded. "Jazz talk to him."

Jazz exchanged her grip on his waist for one on his collar, stared into his eyes and smiled. Her eyes glowed a bright red, her canines grew by inches, hair sprouted on the bridge of her nose, and a growl rumbled up from deep inside her. The vandal's arms and legs began to flail about as he struggled to flee. Jazz caught him by the throat and lifted him off the ground.

"No, no, I'll tell you. Please don't hurt me," he cried.

Jazz set him back onto the ground and released her hold on him.

"Run and you die, punk," Landry told him. "She's even faster when she's angry."

"Don't hurt me."

"Then answer my questions," Landry replied. "Who sent you to vandalize my car?"

The culprit blinked, shook his head, and blinked again as he looked around Landry.

"She did," he confessed pointing to the street behind Landry.

A glimmering shape on the far sidewalk blew away like dust on the wind. Landry turned to Jazz.

"Did you see anything?" he asked.

"Nothing I could identify," Jazz answered and fixed the young man with a glare. "I'm going for a look."

"Don't let your friend hurt me," he begged throwing up his hands as Jazz passed by. "There was a woman there, I swear. She just...just...vanished. Please let me go. Turn me over to the cops anything, just get me out of here."

"You act like you've seen a witch," Landry said.

"Anything you say. Just let me go home," he whimpered and began to cry.

"Who is she?" Jazz asked.

"A woman, I don't know her name. She gave me a hundred bucks. Here, here take it," he said digging in the pocket of his jeans. "Please, I'm sorry."

"Okay, kid," Landry said. "Keep the money. We'll make someone else pay for the car. You can go. I hope this has taught you not to talk to strangers. Now, get."

Landry watched the tire-slashing vandal run out of sight before turning to pursue Jazz.

CHAPTER 16

Whatever shadow Jazz was chasing, it was gone before she reached the far side of Derby Street. She paused for a moment to close her eyes and tried to get a sense of which way to go. There was nothing visible, no scent she could detect, but there was *something*—a feeling. It was faint, barely there.

No, not dread, she told herself, *unease, and moving that way.*

She glanced back over her shoulder at Landry. He was headed her way, but she wasn't waiting for him to catch up. The trail she was following would be gone if she waited. She jogged around the corner of Charter Street and onto the path. Jazz was sure Marie had followed the path a short time ago.

Landry caught up and she held out an arm to stop him from drawing alongside. Looking over her shoulder, she put a finger to her lips. He fell in behind her content to let her lead the way. She did seem to be on to something.

The trail went cold when she reached Essex Street. Jazz paused, turned in a tight circle, looked at Landry, and shook her head. Before he could respond, she held up her hand to stop him, then pointed down the road to her left.

"Go ahead. I'm going this way. I have a feeling," he told her starting in the opposite direction."

Landry walked along the sidewalk studying the area. He continued along Essex Street before crossing to stand outside a bookstore. The name of the store, painted in bold script caught his eye. Behind the glass was an assortment of bells, candles, and books of spells. Landry smiled and shook his head.

Johnny you around?

Now where else I'm going to be? Came the answer Landry hoped for.

Think I'll pay these old movie fans a visit. It would be nice if you tagged along.

About time you thought of me for once. Where we go?

Just follow me.

You sure you want to go in dere? Johnny asked

Pretty sure, Landry told him.

Landry lingered a moment longer looking at the window display, before going inside. A little bell tinkled as the door swung open. Behind the counter in the little shop was a dark-skinned woman with black hair tied behind her head in a long tail. She wore a long-sleeved black shirt with the collar turned up and a pair of faded jeans. Her head came up from the book she was reading, and the smile she had prepared for the new customer withered.

"May I help you?" she asked with unmasked distaste.

Ho, how she already know you? Johnny asked.

I'm loved everywhere I go, Now, hush. Landry fired back at him.

"I'm looking for a book on the witch trials," Landry said aloud.

"We have hundreds," she replied motioning to the many shelves crammed with books new and used. "Help yourself."

"This one is rather rare," Landry said walking over to stand opposite her. "It's by Father Paul Poulard. I hear the book's premise is on the controversial side. Do y'all have it?"

"No," she spat out the response. "That book is the worst kind of bigoted, conspiracy theory trash."

"Yes, that's what I heard," Landry said fixing the woman with a stare. "That's what interests me in it. How about Cotton Mather's book *Wonders of the Invisible World*?" Landry asked. "How about the Book of Amêzârâk?"

"I'm afraid not. Perhaps you should try Barnes and Noble"

"Perhaps later," Landry said. "I'll just browse around a bit first."

"I really don't think we have anything you would—" the ringing phone beside her cut her short and claimed her attention. "Ye's ma'am. We do have that book in stock. Yes. I'll be sure to do that for you."

She hung up the phone and turned on a bright smile.

"Feel free to browse our selections," she said suddenly eager to please. "Let me know if I can help you further."

"Thanks, I'll do that."

Landry went over for a look at the tables near the window that were arranged with tiny brass bells and scented candles. He couldn't resist the temptation to test the bells and check the scent of the candles. He could see the clerk's face reflected in the window and tried a few more bells. Leaving the display behind, he casually strolled the main aisle that was lined with more candles and old books. He ignored the bells as he made his way to the rear of the shop.

What dat you thinking? I hear dose wheels turning, but what all the numbers you countin' off all about? Johnny asked.

This shop is too small, Landry answered.

Maybe dat's all da books dey got.

It's not that. I looked over the building from outside. This shop isn't half the length of the building. See those stairs? There's a second floor they keep dark.

How you know dey keep it dark?

The curtains seen from the street—they're painted, probably on wood.

Landry started back toward the front of the shop recounting his steps as he went. Out of nowhere an arctic wind hit him.

Hey, look out, Johnny warned.

A book flew from the shelf hitting Landry in the forehead and driving him back a step. It was followed closely by a second, and a third. Landry tried to ward off the flying books. He felt a hand shove him back just as an avalanche of heavy reference books and a heavy shelf tumbled down inches in front of him.

Landry stepped over the fallen shelf to the next aisle, checked to see how well that shelf was anchored, and continued to the front of the store.

"Clean up on Aisle Two," he said as he walked up to the woman at the counter. "You really should have someone check the other shelves. Somebody could get hurt."

He dug in the back pocket of his jeans and pulled out his wallet. Pushing aside a few bills, he extracted his card and handed it to the clerk.

"In case the woman on the phone wants to get in touch," he said and strolled out of the shop.

***

Jazz shrugged when Landry left her to pursue his "feeling". She was accustomed to him playing wild hunches. Sometimes they even paid off. In any case, it wasn't any more than she had. She kept moving forward and hoping to stumble upon something.

At the next corner, she crossed the street and started along another that she thought ought to run parallel to Landry's course. Midway down the block, the feeling was back. She stopped and tried different directions, zeroing in on a door. She tried the knob—locked. It wasn't a surprise, but it was a disappointment. At the corner of the building, she found a narrow passage between it and the next building. She jogged past overflowing trash cans, reaching the sidewalk on the far side as Landry left the Bell, Book, and Candle.

"Anything?" she asked.

"Books to die for," Landry replied. "You?"

"I picked up something near one of the back doors."

"Come with me," he said waving for her to follow. "I want to check the outer dimensions of this building."

He counted the paces aloud as they walked the passage.

"Yep," he said went they reached the end. "That shop is half the size of the exterior. Show me your door."

Jazz led him to the door, placed her palm against it, nodded and looked at Landry. "You up for some breaking and entering?"

"Not today. They already tried to drop a shelf on me. It might be good not to press our luck right now."

"I think you got some 'splainin' to do. But you can do it on the way to Deacon Sam's. Let's get out of here."

CHAPTER 17

Landry pulled into the driveway at the rear of the house on Franklin Street. He parked beside a black El Dorado and hurried around to open Jazz's door. They walked up to the back door which opened as Landry raised a hand to knock.

"Come in, come in," Sam greeted them, stepping back and waving them inside.

"Thank you," Jazz said leading the way.

"How was your visit to the church?" Sam asked pointing the way through the kitchen to a living room furnished in a bachelor-lives-here style.

"Reminds me of your place," Jazz told Landry.

"My *former* place," Landry said and sighed. "Those were the days, no lace, no frills."

"Watch it, mister," Jazz replied with a laugh.

"Well, for one thing," Landry began. "We learned it's Deacon Sam. Why the hidden title?"

"He's still a cop at heart," Jazz said. "No manners, just jumps right into the questioning."

"Much to my sainted mother's dismay," Landry added. "Sorry."

"No apologies necessary," Deacon Sam said gesturing them toward a sofa covered in brown leather. "I get it. While I'm planning on being sociable, it's not really a social call. I hope I'm not a suspect?"

"Only of being Father Paul's friend," Jazz told him.

"I'll confess to that crime."

"Is it a crime?" Landry asked, warding off Jazz's glare with a smile.

"In some circles," Sam replied.

"I got that impression," Landry said. "Well, almost, the bookshelf missed me by a good two inches. Seems a local bookseller wasn't happy with my reading list."

"I take it you mentioned Father's book. Coffee, tea? I've heard Landry here has an affinity for a particular beer and made provision for that as well."

"You're sure to be declared a saint," Landry said. "I think I will indulge in a pint."

Deacon Sam returned from the kitchen a few moments later with tea for Jazz and two bottles of Guiness.

"Bless you, Deacon," Landry said taking his beer with a clink of bottles. "Forgive my forwardness once again. What do *you* think is going on at the church?"

Sam took a sip and leaned back in his chair. "I've never encountered anything like it before, so all I can truly offer is my unofficial thoughts. At first, I thought it was, I don't want to say "just", because that sounds like trivializing what happened. However, I thought it was a personal attack on Father by people who disagreed with him and his writing."

"And now?" Jazz asked.

"The word "infestation" comes immediately to mind, but there's something else at work there too that's almost too much for me to take in."

"Just for argument's sake, try it out on us," Landry invited him.

"It's not confined to evil spirits," Sam explained. "I might as well just blurt it out. I think maybe there's real witchcraft and...ah...er...vampires involved."

"You notice that we're not laughing," Jazz said. "So, tell us why you think vampires are involved.

"That's simple enough. Father told me. I just didn't believe him."

"What?" Landry said, leaning forward, elbows on his knees and staring at the deacon. "He *told* you?"

"Yes. He said they threatened to make him into one, damning his soul if he didn't kill himself."

"A priest committing suicide," Jazz mulled it aloud. "Now, that's a hell of a way to discredit him."

"Damned if he did, damned if he didn't," Landry added.

"Somehow he thought you offered another way out," Sam told Landry. "That's why he went to see you."

Landry rose from the sofa to pace the center of the room. Jazz and Sam watched him, neither making a sound nor movement to interrupt him. Several minutes later, Landry sadly shook his head, heaved a huge sigh and dropped down next to Jazz.

"Why?" he asked. "Why must I be the one? I'm just a plain as dirt nobody. Why does this always get dumped on me?"

"Cause, you are plain dirt," Jazz said. "You think people are going to dirty up something fancy?"

"Your wife is being facetious, my friend," Sam intervened. "But in a way, she's right. You're real and people trust you for it. I'm willing to bet it has always been that way. Even as a child you were always the cause's face, the group's voice, and the shoulder that everything got dumped on. Am I right?"

"He probably won't admit it to you, but I will," Jazz spoke up. "And you're right."

"Reluctant heroes are the best heroes," Sam said.

"I'm not a hero!" Landry shouted, jumping to his feet.

He looked at them in turn and sat back down.

"I'm a fool," Landry muttered. "And it got Father Paul killed."

"You're wrong on both counts," Sam's steely voice corrected him. "As I understand it, you saved Father. You were his soul's safe way out. I can tell you he didn't mind going—he was probably relieved."

"The voice of one crying in the wilderness," Jazz said, tears welling up in her eyes.

"Exactly," Sam agreed. "It's a thankless job, but

somebody has to do it."

For once in your life, Eddie, shut up and listen, Johnny chimed in.

"Et tu, Johnny?" Landry said aloud.

"Give him hell, Johnny," Jazz said.

"Johnny, who's Johnny?" Sam asked.

"It's a long story," Landry said.

"One more somebody, Landry saved from their mistakes," Jazz explained. "He's dead, but he still hangs around."

"So, he's a ghost?" Sam asked.

"He says he's now my guardian angel," Landry answered. "He's more like a trouble magnet."

Dat what you call dat well aimed shove a while ago? Saved your life and dat's da truth.

"Okay, okay," Landry said. "So, we have vampires. Nothing new about that. Deacon Wayne, what do you know about him?"

"I'm afraid you've lost me again," Sam said. "I don't know a Deacon Wayne."

"That's what Deacon Kevin said," Jazz replied. "*He's* real, I hope."

"Yes, Kevin's a good man," Sam assured her.

"Well, a Deacon Wayne met us as we came out of Father Paul's office," Landry explained. "Although he was probably there the entire time."

"And how did your time in Father's office go?"

"We sort of ran into a friend from New Orleans there," Landry said. "But she wasn't altogether there just a nebulous image of her."

"A specter," Sam said nodding understanding. "Father said they appeared to him too."

"Did he tell you when that began?" Landry asked.

"No, why?"

"Just a hunch," Landry replied, rising from the sofa. If you'll excuse me, I left some things in the car. I'll need them later."

"And the deacon's forgiveness," Jazz reminded him.

"That too. Be right back."

Landry, good to his word, returned moments later with Father Poulard's books. He held them up for Sam to see.

"I sort of borrowed these from Father's office."

"No problem. I've been meaning to remove his personal things. I promised to take them to his sister in Orange. It's north and west of here."

"So, he had family nearby?" Jazz asked.

"Yes, and no," the deacon answered. "Reckoned in miles it's not far, but she might as well be on the far side of the moon."

"Any clue as to why?" Landry quizzed.

"In Patti's words, she's spiritual, not religious. They might be twins, but that's about the only thing they share."

"Did Patti ever appear to him?" Jazz asked, leaning closer to study Sam's face.

She caught the twinge he tried to hide. His answer was slow in coming. The lie was unnatural to Sam's tongue and difficult for him to deliver.

"No."

CHAPTER 18

Landry excused himself from the after-dinner conversation saying he had some reading to do before morning. It was true enough but not the entire truth. He hoped the deacon would open up to Jazz when she cornered him about his lie. He suspected Father Paul had written about his sister, even though he may not have named her. What better reason to trust spectral evidence than firsthand knowledge?

Worked for me, he reasoned.

Tell old St. Pierre somethin', Johnny spoke up. *A book help you catch da rougarou in your town?*

No, but it did tell me how to put an end to that whole business.

Ho, dat was some kinda surprise ending for Magic Mike.

So, can I get to it now?

Mais, I'll just kinda hang around. You know, in case you need me.

Right, you do that, Johnny.

Landry pulled off his boots, propped himself up against the headboard, and opened the book. Skimming quickly over a few of the personal histories of accused and accusers, Landry focused on the trials. An hour later, a thought came to him. He laid the book down across his legs. Several years ago, he read a book called *The Screwtape Letters*. The author likened Hell to a corporation in which everyone was fighting for the next rung up the ladder. Destroying the next guy up while snuffing out the power of those below was how the game was played. The witch trials could easily fit into that mold. The innocence or guilt of those you destroyed didn't really matter. The game might be demonic in nature, but humans play incredibly well on their own.

Charges and countercharges flew between haves and have-nots, that much was true and many an expert has named that as the root cause of the trials. Jealousy and hate are powerful motivators. However, in Landry's experience, there was a third just as powerful and perhaps more common—greed. The trials and witchcraft had not only grown into an entire industry but a way of thinking. "Witch hunt" was synonymous with mass hysteria and the deliberate, wrongful persecution of the innocent to promote one's own agenda. Witches and witchcraft had become the comedic wearing of pointed hats, laughable tales of eating children, and spells that didn't work. The evil witches imagined by Puritans didn't exist, and never did.

And now, they're untouchable, Landry thought.

Like da rougarou, Johnny reminded him. *I tried to help, and you still had a time selling that one.*

It's worse, Landry replied. *At least the spooky Cajuns believed. Christians don't even believe their own book.*

Bon chance, Johnny told him.

With Johnny gone, Landry returned to his book. In his writing, Father Paul embraced an uncommon, literal interpretation of scripture. Witches, spirits, demons and devils were all real to him as were dreams and visions.

"Spectral evidence makes sense, even in our modern times," he wrote.

Colored with the supernatural and the unbelievable as Landry's world was, Father Paul's writing made sense and so did the rejection of it.

"Seeing is believing," Landry muttered to himself, then read the next sentence aloud. "But surely the reason we do not execute witches is that we do not believe there are such things."

"C.S. Lewis, I believe," Jazz said from the doorway.

"Yes, as a matter of fact it is," Landry assured her. "Quoted here by Father Paul."

"I just came in to see if you needed anything: coffee or that stuff you call beer, maybe."

"I should have coffee, but I'm going to have beer. That is if you'll do the honors."

"I will." She produced a beer from behind her back.

"That's why I love you," he said.

"What, you only love me because I bring you beer?"

"No, because you know me so well and *still* bring me beer. How's it going with Deacon Sam, did he level with you?"

"Yes. He's gone to bed. I'll tell you about it in about two hours."

"Two hours? Why then?"

"*You* still have reading to do. *I* have popcorn and *I'm* going to watch an old movie. You wouldn't like it. It has subtitles."

Really? What is it?"

"The 1957 version of the Crucible."

"You're not kidding, are you?"

Jazz shook her head, turned, and swayed away from the door. Landry exchanged Father Paul for Cotton Mather with a chuckle and a big sip of beer. The dark brew was disappearing slowly. The bottle was still half full when the words in front of Landry began to run together. They slipped behind a black curtain, reappeared, and hid themselves again. He felt himself begin to drift toward sleep.

"You're not reading, you're sleeping," Jazz said from the foot of the bed.

Landry shook his head and looked at the clock on the nightstand.

"I didn't hear you come in," he said. "Did you give up on your movie?"

"Movie?" Her brow knit together. "Oh that... Yes," she said, her face brightening.

"Well then, are you coming to bed?"

"In a minute. I'd thought I'd change first."

"I didn't expect you to get in bed fully clo—"

Landry suddenly realized what she meant. Jazz's head snapped violently from side to side before coming to an abrupt halt with her blazing golden eyes locked on his. Landry knew the look but had never before been the focus of it. Course black hair sprouted from her cheeks and forehead. She drew deep breaths and forcibly blew them out. She jumped onto the bed, long wolf jaws snapping at him. He rolled from the bed, pressed himself against the wall, and sidled toward the door. The rougarou turned tracking his movement.

"Jazz, what are you doing?" he asked, his voice a husky whisper.

A clawed hand cut the air and etched a jagged line across his chest. Blood oozed from the wound staining the hand Landry used to cover it.

"Jazz, stop," he ordered.

She crouched, launched herself at him, and pinned him to the floor. Her transformation to rougarou slowly subsided. Her natural face reappeared although the rage written on it remained. That murderous look went through him like a spike nailing him in place.

Jazz rose to stand over him. A triumphant smile replaced the homicidal rage. Landry felt the breath suddenly sucked from him. Gasping, he clawed at his throat. A sledgehammer blow slammed into his brain. His arms and legs flailed out of control before going limp.

"Now, we are truly one," Jazz told him, pulling him to his feet and shoving him across the room.

Landry stumbled, caught himself and staggered into a chest of drawers. Steading himself, he looked up and saw his reflection in the mirror. The rougarou that stared back at him growled.

"Noooo!" he screamed backing across the room.

He turned toward the laughter behind him, but no one was there. His hands were back to normal. He spun to look in the mirror. Ed Landry was back. He jumped, startled by the sound of the bedroom door flung open.

"Ed, what's going on in here? Are you alright?" Jazz asked, bursting into the room.

Panting for breath, Landry slid down the wall to sit on the floor. The hand he put to his chest came away clean. His shirt was as whole as ever. Except for the day's growth, his face was smooth. Jazz reached out to help Landry up just as Deacon Sam, wearing a robe and rubbing his eyes, appeared in the doorway. Landry held out his hand, quickly withdrew it, and poked her with his finger before accepting her help.

"Is everything alright?" Sam asked.

"No, I don't think so," Landry answered.

"Ed, you're shaking," Jazz said. "What happened?"

It took him several moments to answer.

"I'm not sure but I think I just found the answer to an old problem," Landry said. "But let's go in the other room to talk about it."

"Okay, spill it," Jazz commanded when they were seated and sipping coffee in Sam's living room.

"I was reading Cotton Mather," Landry began. "He believed in spectral evidence but only as a last resort and opposed its use at the witch trials. The big question of the day was could the devil take on the shape of an innocent person?"

"And you know the answer," Jazz said.

"Yes, that is unless you were in the room with me before you came through the door."

"I need a little help here," Deacon Sam said.

"Me too," Jazz added.

"Jazz, or what I thought was Jazz, was in my room moments ago. She clawed me, and I…er…well…I…ah, screamed."

"I'm still lost," Sam replied.

"It was a specter that looked, and I mean *really* looked, like Jazz. That is unless she's in cahoots with the devil. You're not, are you dear?"

CHAPTER 19

Landry cleared away the breakfast dishes and refilled everyone's cup. Sam had invited Kevin to join them and filled him in on all that had happened.

"I thought we might need all the help we can get," Sam explained.

"It usually works out that way," Landry replied. "No offense, Kevin, but the way things went last night, it's going to be hard to know who and what to trust."

"And you're wondering if I'm up to the challenge," Kevin said. "That's fair enough. It's also very honest, so I'll be honest with you. I don't know if I'm up to it. I am willing to do my best. You can count on that."

"We will be," Jazz answered. "It's reassuring that you refrained from boasting about being ready."

"There is one more person I want to add to our group," Landry said. "Rev. Harris Goode, you know him?"

"We've met," Sam replied. "We don't necessarily see things eye to eye, but he's a good man. No pun intended."

"I've never met him, but I wonder if his name worries anyone else?" Kevin asked. "I mean if what you're saying is true, it seems to make sense that those among the first to be accused really were witches."

"And Sarah Good was one of them," Landry finished the thought. "I agree with you, but Harris Goode is no witch. That he might harbor a prosecutory zeal bothers me."

"My husband's choice of words brings up a point I

think we need to emphasize from the outset," Jazz said. "There will be no attempt at prosecution of anyone on the other side for Father Paul's murder. This is going to be strictly an Old Testament solution."

"But what about—"

Landry held up a hand to stop Kevin. "We're not talking about those playing at witchcraft. We're not even talking about true practitioners who keep to themselves. Personally, I don't buy the idea of "white" witches, but that's beside the point. Those we are dealing with here have killed and are causing harm to others."

"There are Christians that harm others," Kevin replied.

"There certainly are. I've arrested a few of them in my time. However, no one questions their existence. *They* can be tried in a court. As for their actions that are immoral without being illegal, well, there's an eternal judgment for those. I'm good with that. Is that being judgmental? Yep, but you can't go through life without making judgments of some kind, no one can. I'm willing to stand before God with mine. How about you? Are you still in?"

"Yes, I'm still in," Kevin mumbled.

"You don't sound very sure," Jazz said. "Why don't you spend the day in Father Paul's office and meet us this evening for dinner."

"That won't be necessary," Kevin quickly replied. "I get your point."

"Do you?" Jazz shot back. "I think you're just scared."

"Of course I'm scared."

"Good. Now let this," she said tapping his chest. "Not your fear lead you."

"Not placing mouse traps is not a humane gesture when you do not believe in mice," Sam told him.

"I read that somewhere," Landry replied. "Or something to that effect."

"Lewis, right?" Kevin asked.

"Yes, and on a subject near and dear to us at the moment," Sam answered.

"Okay, so what do we do now?"

"We start a witch hunt," Landry said with a chuckle.

***

Landry pulled into the small parking lot that ran alongside a frame building covered with beige siding. The structure could have passed for one of the houses that lined the adjacent blocks except for its many arched red, blue and gold opaque plexiglass windows that dotted the front half of the building. He and Jazz walked around to the front of the building. A large wooden cross hung above the double doors and the sign proclaimed it the Salem Church of God, Rev. Harris Goode—Pastor.

Landry tried the door, frowned and looked at his wife. "Locked."

"Probably a good idea in this neighborhood," she replied. "Let's walk around to the other side."

OFFICE read a small metal plaque on a door near the rear of the building. Landry knocked and turned the knob without waiting for an answer. The door stuck a bit but opened up onto a 4x4 square anteroom with dark paneling and equally outdated linoleum on the floor.

"Come in," Goode's voice called from inside seconds before the reverend's face peeked around the corner. "Mr. and Missus Landry, good to see you again."

"I hope we're not intruding," Jazz said. "We tried the front doors."

"A shame we have to keep them locked, but we're a small congregation and have had to replace microphones and musical instruments twice this year. I just made a pot of coffee. Would you care for a cup?"

"Love some," Jazz said, hooking her thumb in Landry's direction. "And he's never turned down coffee in his life."

"Great, step into my office."

Goode waved for them to follow him. Two steps led up from the anteroom to a large combination dining room and kitchen. An abrupt turn to the right and through an open door was Goode's office. In the far wall was another door, this one closed. To their left was an old desk cluttered with papers and a large bible behind which was a wall of crowded bookshelves and a small wooden table that held a coffee maker and a mismatched assortment of cups.

"I moved it in here last month," Goode said pointing at the coffeemaker.

Landry thought the statement rather odd but said nothing. Still, he couldn't help but think there was a reason other than convenience for the move. There was neither water, filters, nor coffee in the room.

Dat's one lazy preacher man rat dere, Johnny said offering his take on the possible significance of the location.

I don't think so, Landry replied.

"Yeah, I don't think so too. Ask him.

"Strange place for a coffee pot," Landry said.

Goode gave him a knowing smile. "We've had...er...problems in the kitchen of late."

"What kind of problems?" Jazz asked.

"Come and see," the preacher said starting for the door.

He pointed to chairs at a long table. "Let's sit over there quietly and drink coffee for a moment, if that's alright with you."

Landry raised an eyebrow in a dubious glance at Jazz. She gave him a weak smile as they took seats across the table from the preacher. Goode seemed to pick up on the look but said nothing. They sipped coffee without speaking for a few moments before Landry's eyes began to wander with a growing sense of purpose. Exactly what he was searching for, he couldn't quite pinpoint. He turned his head just enough to see Jazz was doing the same thing. Landry tried to rub away the feeling creeping up the back of his neck.

"It was here before I took the church," Goode, seeing their growing restlessness, told them. "It's been getting worse—much worse. I've been doing everything I can to avoid this room. It's everywhere in the building, but more powerful here in the fellowship hall."

"What is it?" Landry asked.

"More to the point, why are you avoiding it?" Jazz added. "You don't strike me as the type to let things ride, especially if things are getting worse."

"You're right about that," the preacher said. "The only thing I can say is that I feel the timing is wrong."

"No time like the present," Landry said.

"I disagree," Goode was quick to reply. "Elijah faced down Ahab and his prophets only to run from Ahab's queen. For my money, the difference was that he had no command from God to take on Jezebel. To fully answer your question, I think we are dealing with an evil spirit, and I don't want to battle it without a word from God."

"I'll buy that," Landry conceded.

"How do you think this is linked to the story you shared with us?" Jazz asked.

"As I said this presence predates my arrival. However, I have a theory."

"Let's hear it," Landry said.

"I dug into the history of this church. It's only about thirty years old. That's little more than the blink of an eye in Salem," Goode said, shifting in his seat.

"Constant contention and strife pretty well sum up those thirty years."

He paused to look at Ed and Jazz in turn.

"Soooo?" Jazz asked when he seemed reluctant to continue.

"For rebellion is as the sin of witchcraft, and stubbornness is as iniquity and idolatry," Goode quoted to them. "I think the same kind of spirit involved in local witchcraft has found a home here where rebellion and stubbornness are the rule rather than the exception."

"Then, why did you take the church?" Landry asked.

"Seriously?" Jazz questioned with a scathing incredulous look. "You of all people need to ask that?"

Goode laughed at the sheepish look that bloomed on Landry's face. When he recovered, Landry held his hand out toward Goode.

"Brothers in arms," Landry said. "Do you have plans for the day?"

"I'll be working around the church, and I live just through that door," Goode said pointing at a door directly across from his office. "You're up to something. What is it?"

"I'm glad you asked," Jazz answered. "Here's what we want you to do."

CHAPTER 20

The next stop was the Deacon's office to meet up with Sam and Kevin. The two men gave a startled jump when the Landrys stepped into the doorway.

"Everything alright?" Jazz asked.

"She said she wouldn't come—*today*," Sam reported.

"It was more the way she said it," Kevin added. We had her on speaker. There was so much hatred in her voice."

"She said she'd come for what she wanted when she was ready," Sam said.

"Who are we talking about?" Landry asked.

"Sorry. Patti Poulard, Father Paul's sister," Kevin apologized.

"Any idea what she might be coming for?" Jazz asked.

"Not a clue," Sam replied with a shake of his head. "As far as I know, she's never been in Father's office or the church. I don't see how she could know what's in either of them."

"Perhaps she has friends," Jazz said. "It's even more likely she's been in that office herself, and you just couldn't see her. However, my money is on that you saw something that looked like her. That's why you lied about her appearing to her brother. Patty's a witch, isn't she?"

"Yes, forgive me for lying to you," the deacon said. "I shouldn't have answered at all."

"Because the confessional is sacred," Landry replied. "I understand. My guess is Patty is the one who delivered the ultimatum to Father Paul."

"You're both very good guessers."

"I like to think he has inside information, but won't admit it," Jazz offered.

"It's possible, even without him being fully aware of the source," Deacon Sam agreed, turning to Landry. "St. Paul called it a word of knowledge. It's probably been going on all your life. It just seems normal to know things without really knowing how you know them."

"Or I'm just a good cop," Landry countered.

Ho, now dat's a good one rat dere, Johnny broke in with a laugh.

Landry tried to ignore the jab, but when he looked at Jazz, he could see she caught it. She smiled at him and slowly shook her head.

"Thanks to Rev. Goode, we've had a change in plans since breakfast," Jazz announced. "You've just confirmed the soundness of his words."

"He has a problem akin to the one in Father's office," Landry picked up the thread of the conversation. "He hasn't done anything about confronting it because he has no word from God."

"I feel much the same," Sam said. "So, what are you thinking?"

"Well, I respect that. I understand where you're coming from," Landry answered, nodding his head. "I, on the other hand, take a priest dropping dead at my feet as a sign from God that I must *do* something. There is one thing I want to hear from you two."

"And what's that?" Sam asked.

"If you're directly confronted in your own church, will you fight?" Landry asked.

"I'm not sure what you mean by fight," Sam answered, holding up his hand to forestall Landry's comments. "The way I see it, the thing in the priest's office can't stay there. What happened to Father Paul can't be allowed to happen again. Maybe, your arrival is the word from God that we've been seeking. I don't look forward to it, but I'm ready to clean house."

"Good, your counterpart across town feels the same way," Landry replied. "Are either of you fans of horror books or movies?

"Not me," Sam said looking at Kevin.

The younger man simply shook his head.

"Is there something we should know in them?" Sam wanted to know. "Silver bullets, crucifixes, maybe?"

"Crucifixes do work," Landry said. "But that's not what I'm getting at. Most of what people know about the supernatural comes from fiction whether it's books or movies. That it's nonsense doesn't matter. The supernatural side has a similar blind spot that just happens to turn up in the same sources."

"Blind spot? What kind of blind spot?" Kevin asked.

"That priests, preachers, and deacons are cowards who don't really believe in God," Landry said. "Your faith is all talk and no threat."

"Let them think it," Jazz added. "Until you can spring the truth to our advantage."

"Okay, if you say so," Sam agreed.

"At one o'clock, we want the two of you to go into Father Paul's office and begin to pray."

"That's it, just pray?" Kevin replied.

"Yep, and keep at it until you hear from us," Landry said. "Use those acting skills?"

"What will you be doing while we're acting?"

"While you have their attention, we're going in the front door," Jazz explained. "From there on, we play it by ear."

"You're assuming the shop you went to yesterday and Father's office are connected. What if they're not?" Kevin asked.

"That's where the play it by ear part comes in, am I right?" Sam asked.

"Well, that's one way," Jazz said with a smile.

"And that's your entire plan?" Kevin asked, his voice choked with worry.

"No," Landry said. "The plan is for Jazz and me to go into the shop, brush past the clerk, get upstairs, kill Wilson—"

"If he can be killed," Jazz added.

"Then, we grab the Book of Amêzârâk from whoever's left, destroy it, and escape unscathed," Landry finished. "But the best laid plans and all that."

"The name Amêzârâk sounds familiar," Kevin said turning to Sam.

"It's from the Book of Enoch. He was one of the Watchers. Amêzârâk taught all the conjurers and root-cutters, but I've never heard of a book."

"This Wilson fellow," Jazz began. "Who went by Clemenceau at the time, found it in Louisiana not long ago. He had put together a pack of rougarous—"

"Wait a minute, rougarous?" Kevin interrupted.

"Werewolves," Sam interjected.

"Right," Jazz resumed. "Landry and I tried to get the book from him, but things went…er…ah…wrong."

"You think he's making these rougarous here?" Kevin asked.

"No, something worse," Landry said. "The book has to do with witchcraft, voodoo, magic arts, conjuring, that kind of thing. There is a spell that can be used to create rougarous, but he doesn't need the book for that. Trust me on that one."

"I think it fair to warn you," Jazz cautioned. "There's a woman named Marie Dupree working with him. She's the Queen of Voodoo in New Orleans. She will stop at nothing to get her hands on the book. So, watch your backs."

"We'll leave you with that," Landry announced. "We've got to move if we want to get to the book shop on time."

They parked three blocks away, gathered their

supplies and set out for the bookshop. The sun was a bright spot behind the blanket of gray clouds that hung over the city. The light wind added a bite to the air. On their walk to the back of the bookshop, their eyes scanned the sidewalks and buildings alert for anyone who seemed to be paying them undue attention. Seeing no one, they shared a kiss outside the shop's back door.

"Remember, an unbroken line," Jazz reminded him.

Landry nodded, pulled one of the cardboard containers from his bag, pulled up the metal spout, and set off at a slow walk, pouring the contents as he went.

When it rains, it pours, he thought as he turned the corner. I hope this works.

Oh, ye of da lil faith, Johnny told him. *You da doubtin'est Thomas I ever knew.*

Humor me, Landry shot back.

With another turn of a corner, Jazz came into view as they converged on the front door of the Bell Book and Candle. Less than thirty feet separated them when a young man stepped out of the shop, froze in horror in a moment of recognition, and ducked quickly back inside.

"That was the little vandal from yesterday," Landry said. "So much for the element of surprise."

Jazz poured a neat line of salt to connect with Landry's. "They got nowhere to run."

"After you, madame," he replied opening the door for her.

The shop appeared to be deserted. It wasn't. It was inhabited by millions of creepy crawlers that danced up and down Landry's skin raising gooseflesh on his arms.

"You might as well come out," Landry said.

"We're not going away and peeping at us from your hidey-hole doesn't frighten us," Jazz added.

They were answered by the sound of a door opening at the rear of the shop. The clerk from Landy's last visit came toward them followed by her tire-slashing friend.

"I told you we don't have the books you want. Go away," the young woman said.

"I'm looking for a different book this time," Landry told her. "I'm sure it's here. Perhaps if I could speak to the manager..."

"*I'm* the manager," the man said.

Landry chuckled and shook his head. "Boy, you're not even a good vandal. Go get Mr. Wilson for me."

"If he's unavailable, Marie Dupree will suffice," Jazz added.

"I don't know who you're—" the clerk began.

"It's alright, Val," Marie said from the still open doorway. "We're old...ah...acquaintances."

"That's one way of putting it," Jazz said. "Aren't you worried things will go awry while you're away from New Orleans?"

"Not really. Besides, I plan to be going back very soon."

"Oh, you mean you already have what you came here for?" Landry asked.

"Not yet," Marie said with a fake pout.

"Marie, we need you back here," a tall, shapely beauty with auburn hair called from the doorway. "Now, please."

"Trouble, Marie?" Jazz asked.

"I'm sure it's nothing," Marie answered turning to go. "Valerie is correct, however. The book you're looking for is not here."

"Do we take her word for it?" Landry asked.

"We never have," Jazz replied.

"You're right. I'm sure Marie won't mind us having a look for ourselves."

"You can't just come in here and—"

Landry stepped forward and laid his finger on

Valerie's lips. She pushed his hand away. His hand caught her shoulder, and he shoved her aside.

"Run," Valerie shouted, bolting for the front door.

The young man led the way as they ran the length of the counter. Jazz and Landry smiled at each other as they turned to watch the couple flee. The man yanked the door open, stepped around it, and suddenly stopped, frozen in place. Pinwheeling his arms to keep his balance, he teetered on the threshold.

"What's the matter with you? Go, Charlie," Valerie yelled, planting both hands in his back and shoving him through the opening.

Charlie stumbled out, crashing onto the sidewalk. He began writhing on the concrete, a cloud of yellow smoke smelling of rotten eggs replaced the screams coming from his mouth. Flames burst from his eyes, the air crackled and he was gone.

Valerie took a step back and collided with Landry. She wheeled about with a gasp.

"Poor Charlie," Landry commiserated.

He caught the clerk by the shoulders and pushed her toward the door.

"No, please. Have mercy," she cried.

"How many more like you and Charlie in here?" Jazz questioned.

"None, I swear," Valerie pleaded.

"In that case, we don't need you, do we?" Landry said moving closer to the door.

"Wait! Okay, two more in the back."

"Let's go see," Jazz said.

CHAPTER 21

Rev. Goode found he had suddenly tapped into something beyond his experience. He felt God when preaching and often when praying, but nothing like he did at that moment. He began to pace, spurred on by a feeling of power. His prayer climbed to his preaching volume.

Suddenly, he fell silent. Sometime during his prayer, his feet had carried him into the church. He stood before the altar looking over the church. Something had changed. He felt it though everything looked the same. From the eerie silence came the feeling of a presence. A black mist seeped through the wall, growing as it advanced to tower over him. Hands with long claws formed in the cloud and the makings of a face began to form in the swirling mass. Red eyes glared down as muted laughter floated from the cloud. Goode stood tall and stared back unafraid. The feeling of strength that drove his prayer was silent, but still with him.

"In the name of Jesus Christ," he spoke in words as hard as steel. "I command you to leave this place."

Wind brushed his face, the church doors rattled behind him, and he was alone. Not knowing what to do next, he returned to the kitchen and sat in silent prayers of thanks. His mind soon turned from prayer to thoughts of wonder at what had happened. He was no stranger to the mysterious workings of the power of prayer. It was one thing to believe in the power of God and feel the confidence that came with it. It was quite another to experience it on the scale he had just been surrounded by.

How did Landry know? he asked himself. *Assuming, of course, Landry actually did know. That's a rather big assumption, isn't it? Maybe.*

Goode looked at his watch and laughed.

On second thought, it might be more than secret knowledge. Maybe Landry's the cause, like dropping a little soda in vinegar. One thing's for sure, it's not a coincidence that this spiritual confrontation happened today of all days.

Words of thanksgiving on his lips, Goode went to his office, returned his coffee maker to the kitchen counter, and brewed a fresh pot. He was pouring a cup when that eerie feeling of another's presence crept over him again.

"That's a bit premature, Reverend," a woman's voice spoke from behind him.

With a sharp breath, Goode spun around, his hands holding tight to the counter at his back. A raven-haired beauty with skin the color of red earth and eyes of pale ice stood only a few feet away.

"Who are you?"

"My dear Harris, don't you know? I'm hurt. Don't you remember me?"

"You're not real," Goode insisted.

"Why? Because I come in your dreams," she replied. "Is that so hard to accept?"

"You're a lie, told by something in a bad dream."

She gave him an impish smile. "Now who's lying. They were very good dreams even if they ended in a little needless embarrassment for you. Everyone deserves a fantasy. I'm yours."

"No, no, it can't be. That's not true."

"His left hand is under my head, and his right hand doth embrace me. You remember, don't you?" I can see it on your face

"Blasphemy!" Goode shouted.

"Truth, Preacher," she whispered, sliding seductively closer.

Goode groped behind him for the knife that was there. His hand closed on something metal.

"Stay away from me, witch," Goode demanded.

"I'm no witch. Witches serve me, you know it's true. You serve me and now we shall be together, forever." Her soft hand stroked his cheek as her lips moved to meet his.

"Then, die," he hissed and drove the scissors into her chest.

Rev. Goode opened his eyes to find himself sitting on the floor, his back propped against a kitchen cabinet. His right hand felt like it was on fire. He brought his hand up to examine it. The skin from the tip of his index finger to the tip of his thumb was bright red with yellow blisters where there was skin left. He pushed himself up with his good hand and staggered to the sink. Wetting a clean dish towel, he laid in over the burn.

Mercifully, the woman was gone.

If she was a woman and if she were really there to begin with, he thought.

His wounded hand told him such thoughts would get him killed. She may not have been human, but she *had* been there—that was real. Moreover, she or something like her would be back. The realization sent a shiver down his spine. He was no coward, but he was scared—and hurt. He needed an Emergency Room, but Landry told him to stay put until he sent word. Running out now could endanger everyone involved.

In his bathroom medicine cabinet, there was painkiller left over from his last dental visit.

It's probably expired, he reminded himself.

"I'm trying it anyway," he said aloud. "Stay safe Landry."

He hurried from the room, snatched the bottle from the bathroom and ran back, praying all the while. He placed the bottle next to the sink and got a glass of water. He looked down at the childproof cap, shook his head, and gritted his teeth. Steadying the bottle with his burned hand, he pressed on the cap with the heel of his palm and rotated his hand. The cap was stubborn, but it twisted free.

"Take one or two every four hours," he read from the label.

He shook four out onto the counter. Scooping them up, he chased them with water. He sat down at the table and earnestly prayed alternating between a prayer for the pills to work and one for Landry's success.

An hour later the pain had dulled a little. His hand had swelled to almost twice its normal size. The ringing phone startled him. He jumped and the pain flared in his hand. Goode stumbled into his office and snatched the phone.

"Landry?" he asked.

"No, it's—"

"Help me," Goode groaned, and his world went black.

He awakened as the stretcher bearing him slid into the ambulance.

"No, don't move me," he told the paramedic leaning over him. "I've got to stay here until Landry calls."

"I don't know who Landry is, but you need medical attention. Some guy who said he's Deacon Kevin told us to get you help."

The ambulance lurched, started moving, and the argument seemed pointless. Goode closed his eyes, briefly wondered what he was going to tell the doctor and prayed for the best.

CHAPTER 22

Deacon Sam looked at his watch and then up at Kevin. He felt sure the resignation on his face conveyed the message, but he spoke it anyway.

"It's time."

Kevin held up the bottle he carried and nodded. "Into the breech," he said.

They made their way to the priest's office said a Hail Mary and opened the door. Sam looked at his companion and arched an eyebrow in surprise. All was quiet within.

I'm not sure what I expected, but this isn't it, he thought.

Kevin, seeming to pick up on the thought, shrugged and stepped inside. "Now what?" he asked.

"The hardest thing of all—we wait," Sam told him.

"For what?"

"I'm not sure, but I feel sure we'll know it when we see it. You can bet on that," Sam said.

They settled into the chairs facing Father Paul's desk and began to pray silently. As agreed upon, they prayed first for divine protection and then for the spiritual strength to do what they had come to do. After some minutes, Sam felt a quiet peace come over him. He opened one eye, then the other to find Kevin looking at him. He stood and motioned for his companion to join him. He poured the holy water they brought into the bowl holding the aspergillum. Taking the little polished brass wand, he sprinkled the water on Kevin as he prayed. The blessing was given to Sam a moment later.

"Let's begin here," Sam said pointing at the desk.

Keving nodded in agreement. He held the bowl as Sam sprinkled the furnishings before moving on to the walls. When they reached the bookshelves, Sam took care to sprinkle each shelf.

"Let the mighty power of the Holy God be present in this place to banish from it every unclean spirit, to cleanse it from every residue of evil, and to make it a secure habitation for those who dwell in it; in the Name of Jesus Christ our Lord."

Before Sam could say the "Amen", there came the faint sound of a distant wailing. The entire wall of books began to shimmer, fading from focus. The deacons took a few steps back and the wall seemed to solidify a little.

Tell dat boy go to dother church, a voice told Sam.

"What did you say?" Sam asked.

"I didn't say anything," Kevin replied.

"You said something about the other church," Sam insisted.

"I didn't," Kevin was equally adamant in his denial.

What you wait for? Tell him go, came the voice again.

The voice seemed real enough, but Kevin's lips didn't move. Furthermore, Sam didn't believe Kevin capable of speaking with that atrocious accent.

"Go call Rev. Goode. Hurry, something's wrong."

"I can't leave you," Kevin protested.

"Go!" Sam shouted at him, punctuating the command by stabbing a finger toward the door.

Kevin ran from the room. Sam turned back to face the faint image of the book-covered wall and shook his head. He took a step closer, then another. A vicious guttural growl rumbled a warning. He stopped and squinted, straining his eyes to see through the shifting, swirling scene before him. He took another step and was engulfed in a bright mist. Glancing over his shoulder, he clearly saw Father's office. The aspergillum he didn't remember dropping was lying on the floor behind him. Kevin rushed through the office door. A confused look stole over him, and he shouted words Sam could not hear.

"I'm here," Sam called to him.

Seeming not to hear, Kevin turned and disappeared into the hall. Shouting for him to stop, Sam whirled to go after him and slammed into something hard. A picture of Marcel Marceau sprang into his mind as he explored the barrier he could not see. A sudden chill of terror ran through him that his nervous laugh could not dispel. He was alone.

Lost and alone, he told himself.

Kevin was gone and his retreat to the safety of the church was cut off.

God only knows where Land—" he stopped mid-thought and bumped his forehead with the heel of his hand. Stop it, you may not know where you are, but you're not lost. Don't let fear do the thinking here.

That voice was no devil. That was God's direction. The devil would not send Kevin to Goode's rescue.

With no retreat available, there were only two options stand still or press on.

Let's see, there's stand still and see the glory of the Lord. But there's also go ye into all the world. Forward it is.

The way forward was like walking through a smoke-filled room without all the gasping and choking. He could hear things moving on either side of him. Shuffling, squishing, claw dragging things grunted, growled and moaned, that was bad. Worse was how those things *felt*. They charged at him, clawed at him, loomed over him and always just beyond his sight. The skin on his neck and arms felt like an insect parade ground.

He was sure the room, hall, whatever it was must come to an end somewhere, but the end eluded him. The space had a dream-like quality that seemed to stretch it with each step he took. Something large growled in his ear. He could feel the thing's hot breath on his face. His head snapped toward it.

Nothing.

Why are we always so quick to look at what we don't want to see?

The thought had barely formed when he collided with a door.

I've come his far, he told himself and reached for the door.

The latch turned freely. Sam pulled the door toward him, slipped around it and into—a meadow. A fat silver moon hovered above a ring of tall trees washing the scene in soft light. He jumped and whirled around when the door slammed closed behind him. Without bothering to check to see if it was locked, he stepped out under the clear star-studded sky. The ground was soft underfoot. When he reached the middle of the small clearing, he turned about searching for a clue as to what to do next.

A mournful howl built to a crescendo and slowly faded away. The sound chilled him. He shook it off. He didn't want to run into whatever made the sound, but when you're seeking a sign, you took whatever came your way. Passing through the clearing, Sam came to a path that led into the woods.

Following the path, he wound his way through the trees until he felt utterly lost and sat down on a stump to rest. The woods were strangely quiet. No birds were singing in the trees, no insects buzzed around him. A soft footstep in the leaf litter was followed by another. Something was coming. Sam took refuge behind a fallen tree. As the footsteps drew near, he peered over the log. A gray wolf passed by, paused, looked back at Sam, and continued on its way.

Sam left his hiding place and followed the beast to an Indian village. It circled an oval hut fashioned of saplings and small branches several times before coming to a halt facing the entrance. A tall man stepped out, knife in hand to face the wolf. The beast coiled its muscles, growled a warning and sprang at the man carrying him off his feet. The fight was quick and bloody. When it ended the man lay in his own blood and the wolf limped away bleeding from a wound in its side.

Sam ran to the hut. There was no saving the man. He looked inside at a woman and small child cowering at the back of the structure. The woman screamed at the sight of him. Arms sheltering the child, she pressed herself into the wall. Sam snatched the bow from her hand and a pair of arrows. Turning quickly, he left them and went in search of the wolf.

He followed the trail of blood. He could hear the animal's labored breathing and knew he was closing in on it. He had never drawn a bow in his life but was determined to put an arrow through the wolf's heart. The chase ended in a clearing where a dozen women were gathered. The wolf turned to face the deacon as he raised the bow, nocked the arrow, and drew it back.

The wolf rose onto two legs. As Sam stared at it, the animal became a woman. She held out her arms in welcome.

"Don't be afraid," she told him.

Sam let the arrow go. It hit her chest with an audible thud and a spray of blood. An abyss opened under Sam and he fell.

CHAPTER 23

Meeting resistance with every step, Jazz pushed Valerie down the aisle toward the door at the rear of the shop. Landry tensed as he watched Jazz roll her shoulders. Her head twitched side to side. He couldn't see her face, but he knew she was changing and slowed his pace.

Dat looks like da door, Johnny spoke up. *Mais, dat's a fan and da merde bout to hit it. Better duck, Eddie.*

Way ahead of you, Landry told him, stepping behind a shelf of books.

The Valerie-demon reached for the door, dropped her human covering and whirled around bringing the sharp claws of her right hand toward Jazz's head. Jazz blocked the blow with her forearm. Arms crossed like swords, the two strained against each other, strength against strength. Jazz caught the demon's free hand, relaxed her arm holding the demon back—and pulled as she dropped under the demon. A well-placed foot in the demon's midsection launched it down the aisle. It came to a sliding stop a few feet before reaching Landry who toppled the bookcase atop it.

"Payback," Landry said.

Doan tink so. Get back, Johnny warned.

Landry jumped back. He retreated a couple more steps before the shelf flew into the ceiling. Landry threw his arms over his head as a shower of tiles, splinters, and books descended. The demon, on its feet again, charged at Jazz. The collision carried Jazz and the demon into the air and crashing through the door, ripping it from the frame. Jazz hit the floor with a loud umph. The demon scrambled up and kept running.

A moment later, a rectangle of light appeared around the silhouette of the demon. The Valerie demon had learned its lesson. It saw the waiting line of salt, slammed the door closed, and retreated up a nearby staircase.

Landry helped Jazz up, brushed her off, and held her at arm's length looking her over. He drew her close and gave her a quick kiss.

"You still look beautiful," he told her. "How do you feel?"

"Probably better than I will tomorrow," she replied. She studied his face a moment. "What? What's bothering you?"

"Well, that...ah...thing, it was—"

"Covered with hair," Jazz finished for him. "Yeah, I know. It felt slimy too. So, what's going through that head of yours? Are you worried about me?"

"Yeah, but not like you think, not about trust," he said. "Right now, I'm questioning the wisdom of not breaking the curse already."

"Okay, but we can't do that now. We have a job to do."

"The job doesn't come before you."

"It does today. Trust me," Jazz said looking into his eyes.

"Alright, let's go," he replied pointing up the stairs.

She nodded and took him by the hand. The old wooden stairs creaked and groaned beneath them.

"No surprise, is there?" Landry said.

"Well, we did create a little bit of a stir downstairs. I don't think noisy stairs matter much."

As the room came into view above the last riser, the lights came on and Landry took in a peaceful looking reception party. The room was lit by the soft glow of candles.

"They must be their own best customer," Landry

whispered to Jazz.

In the middle of the room, Marie Dupree sat in a high-back Queen Anne chair covered in red velvet.

"Gaudy, but appros," Jazz muttered under her breath.

"Come in and join us," Marie told them with a wave of her hand around the room. "You've met Valerie. I suggest you hear me out before testing the others."

The trio to Landry's left appeared extremely pale even for northerners.

Vampires. Courtesy of the Casket Girls, perhaps?

The other two demons stood with Valerie behind Marie.

"No witches," Jazz whispered.

"Figures," Landry whispered back.

"No need to whisper. We all hear exceptionally well," one of the vampires said.

"I'm sure you do," Landry told him. "And when I address you, you'll know it."

"Tsk-tsk, Landry," Marie scolded. "That tone is hardly conducive to working together."

"Who said we're working together?" Jazz asked.

"It's in everyone's best interest," Marie replied. "If you will allow me, I'll explain."

"Please do," Jazz said.

"As you know, Clemenceau escaped with the book and is now calling himself Wilson. Do you recognize the connection of the names?"

"A fascination with World War 1?" Landry ventured.

"Not the war, exactly," Marie said. "But the peace that followed and the men who believed they could carve up the world as they pleased."

"With them presiding over it all," Jazz added.

"Exactly. Wilson plans to use the book to carve up the world in his image. He has already started with the supernatural and will work that to shape the natural."

"Like has been done with Salem and witches,

right?" Landry asked.

"Right."

"And nothing can be done to stop it because the supernatural doesn't exist except in the minds of religious fanatics," Jazz chimed in.

"It's a little more complicated than that, but yes," Marie answered.

"Okay," Landry said. "I understand how it's in our interest to stop Wilson. What's in it for you? You get to take his place at the top?"

"Believe me, that's not without its allure," Marie replied with a smile. "But no. I propose to let you have the book."

"Me?" Landry said. "What would I do with it?"

"I would think that was obvious—destroy it," Marie replied. "You may be the only person who would actually do it."

"How does that help you?" Jazz asked. "You don't do something without getting something in return."

"That's true," Marie confessed. "*I* get my own little independent Voodoo kingdom and the undying gratitude of all those struggling to make kingdoms of their own."

"Without the book to help your enemies, there's no one to stop you" Jazz filled in the unspoken reward.

"You could put it that way." Marie gave Jazz a sly smile. "The downside is I'm stuck with the thorn in my flesh sitting beside you. Rest assured Wilson won't let him live. Seems a fair trade to me."

"Unless you can somehow manage to let him destroy the book *and* still get Wilson to kill him," Jazz countered.

"You're assuming, of course, that Wilson is going to lose," Landry said. "He fared fairly well against us last time."

"There is some risk involved for everyone."

"There are two things I need to know up front," Landry said. "Where's the book and how to destroy it."

"I'll add a third," Jazz said. "What is Wilson?"

"Wilson is Nephilim."

"That's just wonderful," Landry groused. "What's the rest of the bad news?"

"The only way to destroy the book is to take it from his hand and burn it."

"Wilson's hand?" Jazz asked.

"Well, the hand of a Nephilim," Marie explained and handed Landry a folded piece of paper. "Read these words before committing it to the fire."

"How am I supposed to get it from his hand," Landry said. "He's not just going to hand it over."

"You're a resourceful man, Landry," Marie said. "You'll figure out some way. But hurry we're meeting him tonight. Meanwhile, a truce?"

Landry rose to go and offered his hand to Jazz. As he did, he looked over Marie's companions.

"Let's call it a *nonaggression* pact," he said, zeroing in on the vampire with the acute hearing.

The vampire gave him a toothy smile and a wink. "Be careful out there."

"We might be the only friends you have left," Marie added.

One of the vampires gasped and jerked as if she had been hit. She clutched her chest and melted to the floor with a crude arrow sticking from her chest.

"Maybe, maybe not," Landry said and waved Marie goodbye.

CHAPTER 24

Their footsteps echoed in the empty church hallway. Finding the deacon's office vacant, they started for the priest's office. Jazz laid a hand on his arm, stopping him before he opened the door.

"Something's not right," she said.

"Yeah, I got that too."

Landry opened the door. A breeze followed them from the hall into the room. They exchanged curious glances and Jazz glanced over her shoulder at the open door.

"Like a vacuum," Landry said.

Jazz nodded agreement. She walked across the room to the desk and picked up the bowl of holy water. Spotting the aspergillum on the floor, she went to pick it up.

"What do you make of that?" she asked.

"They left in a hurry," Landry answered. I don't think they got scared and ran, do you?"

"No, despite Marie's 'only friends left' taunt, they're okay."

"Yeah, that arrow from nowhere—"

The crash of the deacon tumbling from the bookcase cut Landry short. Sam came to a rolling stop with a loud groan. He reached for his bow and began scrambling to his feet before he realized where he was. He glanced over his shoulder at Landry and Jazz and backed away from the bookshelf.

"Wolves are after me," he said keeping his bow leveled at the bookcase.

"It's okay. You're safe now," Landry told him gently

pushing the arm holding the bow down.

"Don't be so sure," Jazz cautioned.

The bookshelf was dissolving into shimmering light. Thundering steps heralded the approach of something monstrous. Sam dropped his bow, slipped the crucifix over his head, held it aloft, and stepped forward to meet it. The steps retreated and the books returned to normal. Sam heaved a sigh of relief and stumbled over to drop into a chair.

"So much for the image of the weakling priest...ah...deacon in this case," Landry said eliciting the tension-breaking chuckle from Sam he hoped for.

"You won't believe where I've been," Sam said.

"Yeah, I would," Landry told him. "And I see you brought back a souvenir."

"I...I...killed a woman."

"I'm not exactly sure how that happened," Jazz said. "But don't let it bother you too much. She wasn't really alive."

"I don't understand," Sam replied. "I saw..."

"We did too," Jazz told him. "We saw that arrow you shot hit a vampire in Marie's bookstore hideaway."

"One less undead creature for us to worry about," Landry added. "Our diversion worked.

"Thank God, you're here," an out of breath Kevin said from the door.

He bent over, hands on his knees panting. Landry went to him and helped him into a chair.

"Catch your breath and tell us what happened."

"Rev. Goode is in serious trouble. He's at Salem Hospital."

"What happened to him?" Landry asked.

"Second degree burns on his right hand," the deacon replied. When we were alone, he told me some kind of demon or something appeared to him. He chased it off and a woman appeared. She was like a ghost at first, but then solid. Anyway, he stabbed her.

Her blood burned him like it was acid. His hand swelled and he passed out. That's how I found him."

"He was in the church's kitchen, wasn't he?"

"Yes. I left him at the hospital. He's supposed to call me when they release him. I had to come back to find Sam, but I see you've done that already. Where'd you go?"

"Through the looking glass, after a fashion," Sam answered pointing at the bookcase.

Jazz walked to the bookshelves and began patting them.

"I don't like the looks of that," Landry said.

"The specter we saw in here came from here," Jazz said continuing to test the shelves. There's a portal here. It can be accessed from this side, but how?"

"A portal? To where? To what?" Kevin fired off questions.

"Into the woods," Sam replied. "But I don't think it's just where. I think it's when too. There was an Indian hut, and the people were dressed like the old Puritans."

"And as we saw," Jazz said. "It's connected to that bookstore."

"It's like the painting mama Lille had," Landry said.

Jazz simply smiled, shrugged, and went back to inspecting the shelf. Exasperated, she planted her fists on her hips and growled. A wide-eyed Kevin backed up a step eliciting a chuckle from Landry. Jazz suddenly whirled around. Landry instinctively threw his arm across Kevin's chest but her attention was elsewhere.

"Sam," she said, "What were you doing when this opened up?"

The deacon held up the aspergillum. "Praying and using this to sprinkle the holy water."

"Would you try it again?"

"If you think it will help."

"What are you doing, Jazz?" Landry asked.

"Thought we would knock and see if anybody

answers," she replied. "I have a plan. We need some cord, rope, something to tie around Sam."

"We have cordage used to reserve seats," the deacon said. "We could tie them together."

"Let's go," Landry urged.

The two men quickly rounded up a half dozen lengths of gold cord. They were back in the priest's office in less than twenty minutes. Landry began tying the cords together while Jazz looped one around Sam's waist. The deacon crossed himself and began to pray softly.

"I'm sure this is about as far from the holy of holies as we can get," Sam said when he finished his prayer. "Still, I hope I'm worthy."

"You'll be fine," Landry told him.

Sam stepped up to the bookshelf, sprinkled holy water, and began the prayer of cleansing. Though the door and windows were closed, a breeze soon began to ruffle the deacon's hair. He visibly shivered but kept praying. Landry tightened his grip on the cord. Kevin rubbed his eyes as if trying to clear his vision as the books and his friend faded.

"Tell us what you see," Jazz ordered.

"Books, but they're blurry. I can't read the titles," Sam reported and vanished into a swirling mist where the shelf once stood. The golden cord seemed to float in midair. Jazz looked at Landry and shook her head. Sam's voice spoke from the mist.

"I can't see you, but I see something up ahead. There are tall trees. The moon, I see the moon. There's a light...a fire. It's the same place."

Landry's mind began to drift to a cabin on the bayou. Sam's scream snapped him back to reality. He pulled with all the strength born of sudden panic. Sam landed on his back in front of the bookshelf with a loud thud. Hand over hand, Landry continued to pull the cord and the helpless deacon toward him.

A shadowy silhouetted form began to emerge from

the mist. Sam dug his heels into the floor pushing himself away. Landry's pulling on the cord kept him off balance. Finally, the deacon rolled over and scrambled to his feet as the mist solidified behind him. Landry caught Sam by the arm.

The face of the thing that stepped from the mist was more reptilian than human. A long, forked tongue slithered from its lipless mouth, tasting the air. Golden eyes with narrow vertical pupils tracked a path from Landry to Sam to Kevin to Jazz. The creature's eye locked onto Jazz. Its tongue flicked rapidly in and out. Its mouth opened wide and two long fangs dropped from the roof of its mouth with a hiss.

Jazz answered with a throaty growl and stepped between the creature and the men. She bared fangs of her own as she slowly advanced on the snake-headed monster. The creature retreated into the mist and a moment later only a very solid bookshelf remained.

"Let's get out of here," Kevin said, starting for the door.

The others followed a few steps behind him, slamming the door closed behind them.

CHAPTER 25

Rev. Goode slowly forced his right eye open just enough to see where he was. The room swam into a blurry sort of focus and his head started to float away. He was still in the hospital, but no longer in the Emergency Room. Thank God the blaze in his hand had faded into smoldering embers.

I suspect morphine played a supporting role in that miracle, he thought. *I need to thank the doctors and nurses too, but not just now.*

Goode struggled to focus on his present plight, knowing to let his mind wander now would bring back the darkness.

Lord knows my thoughts aren't much lighter.

The demon, that's what she really was, he knew that now, had not only invaded his dreams, but stabbed him with feelings of guilt. And it was all a lie. He'd laughed at silly television shows in which wives blamed husbands for things they did in dreams. Then, like a fool, allowed himself to be plagued by the same kind of nonsense. No wonder the thing in the church never confronted him. It was too busy laughing.

No more.

He had dealt the demon masquerading as a witch a death blow. Not that it died, but its hold on him did. He was free.

The truth will indeed set you free.

Lying still, his eyes closed, he reveled in the power flooding into him. But he couldn't lie there forever. Landry and the others were counting on him. He tried in vain to force his eyes open.

So tired. Just a minute longer, just a min...

The gurgling of water tumbling over smooth stones in a little stream reached his ears a moment before he opened his eyes. The hospital was gone. He stood on a narrow path unsure of where he was or how he got there. Tall elms and maples crowded the path and blocked out much of the light. Goode looked down surprised to see a rifle cradled in the crook of his arm. How it got there was a mystery as confounding as his surroundings.

He had to be dreaming. But everything looked—he stooped to pick up a dry leaf and crumbled it in his hand—and felt so real. Through the branches, he could make out the sun low in the sky and directly in front of him. Is that east or west, he wondered and stepped off toward the sun without answering.

He hadn't gone far when he came to a stream. Stepping on stones he crossed without getting his boots wet.

Boots? Where did I get boots?

He shook his head to chase away the question. There were more important things to consider. Like where he was and what he was doing here. One thing he felt sure of was that he would not find answers just standing around. He pushed on, whispering a prayer as he went. One answer became clear in just under an hour. He was headed west, and the sun was going down.

As twilight crept into the woods, the path skirted the edge of a clearing. Goode sat down on a stump to rest. A quick look around confirmed that it was not a natural clearing. The area had been cleared. The trees had been cut—felled by saws, not axes. He wasn't sure what that might portend, but the thought clung to him and refused to let go. The sound of something bounding through the trees drew his eyes and attention to the far side of the clearing in time to see a large buck spring from the trees into the tall grass.

Goode snapped the rifle to his shoulder. Catching the sudden movement, the deer bolted away from a shot that never came. Goode watched along his sights as the animal's white rump vanished behind an elm before lowering the weapon. He had no taste for venison and no desire to kill for sport. It was getting dark. There had to be a town or village nearby. After all, he was out here on foot, even if he didn't recall how he got to wherever here was.

He decided to reverse course in the hope he had been setting out from somewhere rather than walking away. There was no reason behind that thinking, just a feeling. It made as much sense as any of the rest of this. As he rose from his seat, he heard voices. It didn't sound like conversation. It sounded like...like...like, well chanting. It made his skin crawl. He slipped behind a tall oak tree and waited.

A dozen women dressed in plain brown skirts and waistcoats with white aprons filed into the clearing from the east. Their chant faded into what sounded like prayers, but Goode could not make out the words. They gathered around a pile of cut branches, carried them to the nearest edge of the clearing and returned to form a circle around a downed tree.

Something wasn't right. The tree was not round. The top of it was flat. From across the clearing, it looked almost smooth though he doubted that was true. The women laid their hands on the tree, looked up at the sky and resumed chanting. The volume and tempo built over several minutes mesmerizing Goode, drawing his focus down to a pinpoint.

Blinding white light flared behind his eyes. A hollow echo sounded in his ears and the light faded in swirling colors. Goode's strength drained from him, and he sagged to the earth. His vision swam into focus on a familiar face.

"You," Goode moaned.

The raven-haired beauty of his dreams stared back at him.

"But I killed—"

"Killed me?" she finished for him. "Harris, you should know better."

The women came from the dark to stand around them. There was no softness in their faces. Only hunger in their eyes. Goode shivered as they took him by the arms lifting him from the ground. His head throbbed and he pulled a hand free to gingerly probe the lump on the back of his head.

"To the altar," one of the women muttered and the others quickly took up the new chant.

Goode tried to break free, but they held him with hands as strong as iron bands. Fingernails, sharp as claws, tore at his coat and shirt drawing blood. He was thrown down atop the altar they had fashioned in the woods. In a mindless frenzy the women danced around him in a circle and thew their clothes into the air. Most of the words of their chant sounded like gibberish. Those he could make out turned his blood to ice: Apollyon, Abaddon, Lucifer.

Demonic hands, soft as silk and beautiful as those of an angel pulled away what was left of his clothes.

"Azâzêl send your son," she whispered.

"No!" Goode screamed and sat up in his hospital bed.

Moments later, two nurses burst through his door.

"What's going on in here?" one asked as the other scanned the monitor and checked his IV.

"A bad dream," he said mopping sweat from his brow. "I'm okay now."

"That must have been some dream."

"I'll be fine now," he assured her.

"Okay," she said and walked out without looking back. The other smiled sweetly and winked as she left.

Goode's hand went to his chest as a gasp escaped him as he recognized her face. She was one of them. She was there—in his dream. She wiggled her fingers, turned out his light, and walked out.

Shadows stretched over Goode's bed as the sunlight streaming through his window faded into the relative darkness of hospital rooms. There was a metallic click of the door latch. The thin beam of light from the hall quickly grew, and a dark silhouette slipped inside.

"Hello, preacher. Were you worried that I wouldn't be back?" a feminine voice cooed.

The room filled with light. The young nurse, her back pressed against the light switch, smiled wickedly. Her smile abruptly vanished. Rev. Goode was gone.

CHAPTER 26

Landry, and the deacons silently spent a few moments with their thoughts while Jazz made a fresh pot of coffee. Despite his assurances to the contrary, Kevin's hands were still shaking too badly to do the job.

"Come and get a cup," Jazz announced when the brew was ready.

Kevin gave the pot a skeptical glance before lifting it higher for a closer inspection. With an almost imperceptible shrug, he reached for an empty cup.

"Something wrong?" Jazz asked.

"Well, ah...that is...ah, it looks a little strong." The deacon took a sip. His head and shoulders quivered, his mouth drew down into a frown and his eyes grew wide.

"Now, brother, that's coffee," Landry said with a chuckle. "See, your hands have quit shaking already."

"Yeah, now my insides are," Kevin shot back.

Landry gave Jazz a quick kiss and took a seat to savor his coffee. "We need a plan," he said.

"You mean you don't have a plan?" Sam asked.

"Plans go wrong," Jazz said. "We tend to have a general direction in which we try to steer things.

"Beyond that, we fly by the seat of our pants, right dear?" Landry added.

"Right, though mine fit better and are more stylish than yours."

"Okay," Kevin said. "Then, which way are we going?"

"My husband is legendary for charging straight in

like a bull in a china shop."

"Hey, it works," Landry interjected.

"It rarely ever works," Jazz replied. "But in this case, perhaps we can use it to our advantage. Marie and her friends expect us to be focused on Wilson and the book. Then, they'll finish us from behind."

"But not until they see which way things are going," Landry said. "If they see Wilson winning, they won't wait. They'll jump in and help him like good friends are expected to do."

"Realistically, what are our chances against this Wilson?" Kevin asked.

"Well, he is part human," Landry began.

"*Part* human?" Sam asked. "I shouldn't be surprised hearing stuff like that anymore, but I am. *What is* he, then?"

"According to Marie, he's a Nephilim. You're familiar with that term?"

"Of course. The product of angel and human mating."

"But they all died in the flood," Kevin said.

"Yes and no, that is it depends on how it's interpreted," Sam corrected, picking up the Bible from his desk. "Genesis 6:4. 'There were giants in the earth in those days, and also after that, when the sons of God came into the daughters of men.' Some believe the giants of Caanan encountered in the Exodus were the 'also after that' variety of Nephilim."

"How do we beat something like that?" Kevin asked. "Can we beat him?"

"Marie Dupree thinks so," Jazz replied. "It's not enough to get the book from him. He has to be neutralized, or he'll just come after her. So, there is some way. We need to find it."

"Unless destroying the book *is* the means of neutralizing him," Landry suggested. "That could be why she has no plans for the book."

"Assuming she's telling the truth," Sam said.

"There is that," Jazz agreed.

"So, what's our next move?" Kevin asked.

"I think we should check on Rev. Goode," Jazz said. "They are aware of his involvement now and he's out there alone."

"I have the number for his room," Kevin said, taking a slip of paper from his pocket and dialing the phone.

"No answer," he said a few moments later. "He could be sleeping."

"Or he could be in trouble," Landry replied. "I think I'd better go find out for sure."

"What about our meeting with Marie? Is there time?" Jazz asked.

"We leave no one behind," Landry replied. "We've been trying to keep both sides off balance. I'm not sure how well that's working, but we have hurt them. Let them come to us. We will just have to hope I get back in time."

"Where, here?" Sam asked.

"I can't think of a better place, can you?" Landry asked. "We know where their door is."

"You're thinking of ambushing them," Jazz said.

"Sort of. If we force her to come here, Marie will know something's up," Landry explained. "But she will expect to parley first, not an immediate attack."

"A line of salt will cut off her demons," Jazz said.

"And we have two soldiers of the cross to drive off the vampires." Landry added, nodding toward the deacons.

"What about Marie?"

"Perhaps we could have a conversation with her about returning home."

"Okay, go get the preacher, but hurry," Jazz said.

***

Harris Goode struggled to get his wounded hand through the sleeve without crying out in pain. He made it—just barely and was rewarded by a lingering throbbing. He slipped out the door and down the hall, avoiding the nurses' station. As he crept down the stairs, he said a prayer of thanks for his many visits to Salem Hospital.

He reached the lobby as the page for security sounded overhead. He stuffed the bandaged hand into his coat pocket and kept walking. By the time security responded, he planned to be long gone. All was going as planned until he glanced back a few blocks from the hospital. Foot traffic was light on cold February nights. The lone dark figure following him was easy to spot.

He crossed the street three times, and the man did the same. Whoever it was made no effort to close the gap between them or try to hide.

He wants me to know he's there, the preacher thought.

Goode was not a man who was easily intimidated. Nevertheless, he felt a shiver run down his spine that was not related to the frosty night air. He maintained his pace and quit looking back. He would hear the man's footsteps if he got close enough to present any real danger. His concern about being attacked from behind vanished when a very large man stepped from behind a cemetery monument to walk out onto the sidewalk up ahead. The streetlight shining down behind the man sent a long shadow the preacher's way.

Goode stopped for a moment, sighed, and resumed his walk toward the big man.

I wonder if this is how David felt? he wondered.

The man up ahead retreated a few steps so that he was directly under the amber glow of the streetlight. His features were partially obscured by shadow. However, a sharp nose and thin lips drawn down in a tight frown were visible beneath the shadow cast by the brim of his hat.

Footsteps on the sidewalk behind him told him that his tail had finally decided to come closer. Goode came to a halt at what he judged to be just beyond the big man's reach. The frown on the man's face dissolved into a practiced smile as a long thin finger touched his hat.

"Rev. Goode," he said. "My name is Wilson. Are you sure it was wise to leave the hospital without your doctor's permission?"

Wilson's voice was a rich, round baritone that seemed at odds with the man's angular features.

"I found the nursing staff a bit contrary."

"Did you now? It is hard to get good help these days," Wilson replied with a sneer. "That hand must hurt. Lilith really wants you to suffer for that. I can protect you from her."

"What's that going to cost me, my soul?"

Wilson's laugh set a shiver through Goode. "Nothing so melodramatic as that. Just your cooperation in ridding me of this Landry fellow. You can always repent afterward. Meantime there are many pleasures to be had and dreams that can come true."

"Why? What do you have against Landry?"

"He's a nuisance. He disrupted my plans once and means to do so again. He killed my worshippers."

"Is that what this guy behind me is, your worshipper?" Goode asked, jerking his thumb over his shoulder.

"Deacon Wayne? Yes, among other things," Wilson admitted. "I prefer to think of him as a keeper of the flock. Show him, deacon."

Wayne snapped his fingers, and several women materialized from the shadows of the cemetery. They crowded around the deacon. One auburn-haired beauty pressed herself against Wayne's back and wrapped her arms about his waist.

"The last three hundred years haven't all been very kind," Wayne told him.

One of the women approached Goode and reached for him. He pushed her away. "No, thank you."

"Nice try ladies," a familiar voice said. "This one is mine. You hurt me, Harris, but I'll forgive you. If you help us tonight, that is."

"What is it you want me to do that all of you cannot?" Goode asked.

"See, now that's the kind of reasonable attitude I'm looking for," Wilson answered with a smile.

"Give Mr. Wilson a little blood, and I'm all yours," Lilith seductively promised. You won't really be betraying your friend. He's doomed no matter what you choose. It's just so much sweeter this way."

"Come, Reverend, we have an appointment to keep," Wilson said. "You were headed to the church. As luck would have it so are we. Please, lead the way."

CHAPTER 27

Landry heard the bolt hit the stop in the door behind him. He saw movement to his right and hurried down the steps. A group of people were gathered under a streetlight in front of the nearby cemetery. He couldn't make out faces and quickly decided not to wait until he could. He backed up against the church and followed the contour of the wall around the corner. Concealed behind a pine tree, he had a clear view of the front steps.

Rev. Goode was at the head of the group. Though he looked different than he did in Louisiana, the lanky man on Goode's heels had to be Wilson. Bringing up the rear was a face Landry recognized—Deacon Wayne.

So, both sides have been in the church at will. Why am I not surprised?

Landry turned and moved along the building to the only window with a light shining within. Hoping Jazz and the deacons were still there, he tapped out a distress signal on the glass. Jazz appeared at the window moments later.

"Wilson has Goode. They'll be coming in the front door any minute," he said when she opened the window. "Find someplace to take cover."

"What about you?" Jazz asked.

"I'll slip back in behind them. Wait for my signal."

"What signal?"

"I don't know yet," Landry answered. "But you'll know it when it happens."

"I'm sure I will."

Landry made his way back to the shelter of his pine tree as Goode mounted the steps to the church door. He tried the knob without success and followed that with a pair of hard tugs.

"It's locked, guess we'll come back later," Goode told his companions.

"I'm afraid not," Wilson replied and signaled for Wayne to address the problem.

The deacon laid his hands on the knob, there was a flare of red light, and he pushed the door open. Wilson put his hand between Goode's shoulders and pushed him inside. All but two of the women started up the steps.

Lookouts, Landry thought. *Oh oh, good ones too.*

One of the women looked Landry's way and pointed. Both women started toward him muttering words he couldn't make out as they approached. One of them threw an open hand his way. A blast of cold air hit him. He felt his joints begin to stiffen as if he were freezing. He took a step back on legs that wouldn't bend and nearly fell. He made a fist, opened and closed it as he forced his arm behind his back. His hand closed on the weapon in his belt.

A shriek from inside the church drew wicked laughter from the women. Landry brought the gun up and the laughter stopped. Two rapid squeezes, two explosions, and they never laughed again. Landry dashed across the front of the church and up the steps. He stumbled over the body in the doorway and went down.

"We weren't able to head Marie off, Jazz said pointing to the body. "That's one of hers."

"It's the clerk from the store," Landry said standing to his feet.

Jazz rolled the body over. "Kevin stuck a silver crucifix in her eye. Seems demons don't do well will silver or crosses."

"Where are Sam and Kevin now?"

"Hopefully still in Father's office. Right now we have more pressing matters." Jazz pointed toward the altar.

Wilson stood behind the altar with a knife to Goode's throat. A raven-haired woman stood on Goode's other side. Wayne and the others were arrayed in a ring around them.

"Mr. and Mrs. Landry," Wilson greeted them. "Come join us. You seem to have an affinity for this ceremony. I must warn you, this time I will not stand for any interruptions."

"I'd say it's too late for that," Landry replied. "We've already crashed the party."

"On the contrary," Wilson said. "You're just in time to serve as ushers. I believe you have kept the other guests away. Perhaps you can bring them in now. Just you Landry. Your wife can stay and entertain us."

"She can do the trick she did at the last party," Landry countered. "Your other friends thought it was to die for."

"I could show them. This dour bunch looks like they could use a little excitement."

"I assure you the reverend here would not find it so amusing," Wilson said. "Landry, our guests, if you please."

Landry leaned over to give Jazz a peck on the cheek. "I have an idea. I need a distraction when we come back though."

"I love you too, dear," she said so all could hear.

He walked down the hall to Father Paul's office, rapped on the door and called to them.

"Landry," Sam said when he was inside. "It seems our plans went awry rather quickly."

"You adapted well," Landry told him. "Mr. Wilson has requested everyone's presence in the church. I think Marie and her bunch ought to lead the way."

Still holding their crucifixes in front of them, Kevin and Sam moved to allow Marie and the others to pass.

"I'm going to savor your blood," Melissa told Kevin as she went by.

He stabbed at her heart with the sharpened crucifix. Melissa jumped back with a hiss.

"Or finally meet God," Kevin said. "Helping lost souls to find God is what I do."

Sam and Landry were the last to leave the room.

"Do you still have that bow?" Landry asked.

"In my office."

"How about a cigarette lighter?"

"Father's old pipe lighter is in the top drawer. What are you up to?"

"Help me sneak it into the church."

Jazz glanced over her shoulder as Sam turned the corner into the nave. He gave her a quick nod and paused when he reached the aisle. Jazz held out a hand to keep Kevin back as she changed into a rougarou. With a howl, she sprang toward Marie. Her vampire bodyguard met Jazz in midair, and they crashed into the aisle. Claws and fangs flashed.

"Enough!" Wilson shouted.

Jazz returned to human form, the vampire returned to Marie's side, and Wilson smiled as the congregation slipped into their pews. Jazz took a seat across the aisle and glanced at Landry who smiled and nodded his approval.

"And now we reclaim the Book of Amêzârâk," Wilson announced. "And with it the power to rule as gods. Just a few housekeeping items before we begin. Mrs. Landry, Jazz, if you would join your husband and the deacons in their pew.

"It's Mrs. Landry," she said as she started across the aisle. "Jazz is reserved for friends."

"I'm hurt," Wilson mocked, holding a hand over his heart. "Sarah, Rebecca if you two would see to our guests."

Two of the women standing by Wayne left the platform. One walked down the center aisle. The other moved along the wall. They took up places at either end of the pew occupied by the Landrys. Both raised their faces toward the ceiling and began to speak. Not recognizing the words, Landry gave Jazz a questioning look. She shook her head and shrugged.

"No," Sam leaned closer to Landry and whispered.

The women stopped speaking and spread their hands toward one another.

"The spell will keep you confined to your pew," Wilson explained. "We don't want you up wandering around during the ceremony, now do we. I know how you struggle with the temptation to interfere."

The women returned to their places on the platform beside Wayne. When they were in position, Wilson turned his eyes on Marie and held out his hand.

"Marie, my dear, please join us. Some of you have questioned the wisdom of uniting with Marie. But she brings a new perspective, one of open practice. In New Orleans, voodoo is not hidden or the practice denied, it is celebrated. As your witchcraft will soon be here."

Marie ascended the platform to stand beside Wilson.

"We are all disappointed that Father Paul couldn't be here tonight. His blood would have been the icing on the cake. Rev. Goode, we do appreciate you standing in for him. You hand if you please."

Goode broke away from the group. Lilith and Wayne caught him and dragged him atop the altar. While the deacon held him around the waist, one of the women tied his ankles and another bound him to the altar. Lilith slammed his right arm onto the marble. Wilson handed her a golden bowl, placed the book in the center of Goode's chest, and lifted his knife.

As Goode struggled, Wilson drew the knife across the clergyman's wrist. To cries of "Blessed be", Lilith lifted his wrist letting the blood drip into the bowl. The vampires jumped to their feet eyes alive with hunger. Marie threw up her hands keeping them at bay.

"Sacrilege," Kevin shouted.

He tried to climb over the pew in front of him to no avail. Sam was equally unsuccessful at escaping into the aisle near the wall. Wilson held the bowl up. Each of the others walked by, dipped their finger in the blood and drew a pentagram on their forehead. The circle reformed; Wilson poured the blood over the book. Taking the book in both hands, he held it over his uplifted face and with a lion-like roar, let the blood drip into his mouth.

Wilson's eyes glowed with blinding white light. Screeching phantoms flew from the pages of the book and circled the room on a whirlwind. Those in the circle raised their arms to shouts of ecstasy.

A burning light blazed a trail across the room. The book was ripped from Wilson's hands and pinned to the cross behind him by a flaming arrow. Silence, like a bomb, exploded in the room as the book was consumed by green fire.

CHAPTER 28

Jazz growled as the change came over her. She leaped from the pew. Landry dropped the bow and drew the pistol from his ankle. Kevin and Sam filed out of the pew after them as chaos enveloped the church.

Jazz hit the vampires before they could turn carrying them over the pew in front of them. Her claws raked Hamilton's neck and back. Melissa threw Jazz off her friend into the wall. She launched herself after Jazz. Rougarou and vampire grappled in the aisle. Jazz found herself pinned to the floor, Melissa looming over her fangs bared.

The vampire's eyes suddenly went wide. A puff of breath escaped her lips. She went limp and fell. Jazz shoved Melissa off her. Blood streamed from the vampire's lips. Kevin rolled Melissa over and retrieved his crucifix from her back.

A tortured scream came from the altar. Wilson, face still covered with blood, was lifted into the air and dragged into the dying embers that were what remained of the book. His scream died in the round of shots from Landry's weapon.

Hamilton jumped up to confront Jazz but found Kevin between them. He fixed the deacon with a stare willing Kevin to surrender.

"Drop it and face me," Hamilton commanded.

"And of course, when I do, you will drop your fangs," Kevin retorted, pressing closer to the vampire. "I think not."

"Well," Landry quipped from two rows back while stuffing fresh rounds in his pistol. "Tell us again what

what you will do to the cowering man of God."

"You don't have a cross and that gun won't hurt me," Hamilton replied, turning on Landry.

"Let's see." Landry snapped the weapon up, pointed it at Hamilton and squeezed the trigger.

The vampire staggered, gagged, and dissolved into bare bone.

"I smell pizza," Kevin said still staring at Hamilton's remains.

"9mm garlic," Landry said.

"Marie got away," Jazz, back to human form, told them.

"How?" Landry asked.

"What about Rev. Goode?" Kevin asked.

"Sam's taking care of the preacher. I called for an ambulance," Jazz said. "I don't know how Marie pulled it off."

"How are we going to explain all this?" Kevin asked.

"Vandals," Landry said. "Pagans broke in because they thought Father Paul and the church was…I don't know…preaching against them, something like that."

"Weak, Landry," Jazz said. "But they're almost here so it will have to do."

"We could show them the bookshelf," Landry countered. "Introduce them to the lizard."

"I don't think so," Jazz said. "But we need to check it out when they are gone."

A pale Rev. Goode was whisked away with dangerously low blood pressure from the loss of blood. Landry, Jazz and the deacons spent the next three hours answering the same questions multiple times. The Salem police weren't buying their explanations. But faced with the word of two ex-cops and respected deacons of their own church, they relented.

"The night's not over," Jazz said when the police were gone.

"You're kidding," Landry replied. "What now?"

"We have to check on Rev. Goode."

"You're right," Landry said. "Kevin, you and Sam might as well go home and get some sleep. We'll meet up tomorrow…er…later today."

"What about…" Sam tilted his head toward the priest's office.

"Tomorrow," Jazz pronounced.

When Landry and Jazz arrived at the hospital, Goode was still in the Emergency Room. His wound was sutured and dressed. IV fluids were going. A nurse came through the curtain a short time after them.

"Do you know how he was injured?" he asked. "The report of the crew who brought him in seemed a little sketchy."

"It is a little hard to explain," Landry admitted.

"He was abducted. The kidnapper slit his wrist," Jazz explained.

"So, it was not self-inflicted?"

"Definitely not," Jazz assured him.

"Sometimes burn pain can, well, get to be too much. Especially when you sneak out of the hospital instead of waiting to be discharged."

"Yeah, we're not sure why he did that," Landry replied. "But that's kind of why we're here."

"I don't follow,' the nurse said.

"Someone connected with the kidnapper works here," Goode said from his bed. "That's why I left the way I did."

"Well, you're going to be here for a while this time. You need a transfusion."

"Can that happen here in the ER?" Jazz asked.

"I can ask. No guarantees."

"I'd feel better,' Goode told him.

When the nurse was gone, Goode looked up at Landry and Jazz and smiled weakly.

"Guess I wasn't much help," he said. "That Deacon Wayne followed me from the moment I left the hospital. One of the nurses was a witch. I had to get out and make it back to you."

"You did fine," Landry assured him.

"What now?"

"We're not quite sure yet," Jazz told him. "The witches with Wilson at the church are all dead. Likewise, Marie's vampire bodyguards."

"Wilson seems to have been sucked into the ashes of his book. I'm not sure what that means. Marie disappeared in the melee. With the book gone, I'm betting she'll be on the next plane to New Orleans," Landry said.

"When you get out of here, we plan to check both churches to see if there's any paranormal activity still going on," Jazz added.

"What do you think we'll find?" Goode asked.

"One thing is certain," Landry said. "There are plenty more witches active in Salem. Marie had four demons around her. They are still around as well. As for Wilson, it's anybody's guess."

"Is that a yes or a no?"

"It's saying the problem still exists," Landry said. "But you know that. It's unlikely it will manifest at either church again. Their greatest weapon is invisibility. I think they will stick with that for the near future."

"I don't mean to rain on your parade," Jazz spoke up. "There is another way this can go. You could end up like Landry here."

"I'd give you my spot, except I like you," Landry told him.

The nurse pushed aside the curtain and stepped inside. "Excuse me folks, I'm going to draw some blood for a type and cross. We got the okay to transfuse you here."

"Good news," Jazz said.

"It is if there's a coffee fountain close by," Landry quipped.

"I can help with that, and maybe a couple of hard chairs, if you're interested."

"God bless you. By the way what's your name?" Landry asked.

"They call me Jack because I'm a real—just call me Jack.

Jack put bands on Goode's wrist and disappeared with vials of blood Goode probably couldn't spare.

"It's takes a bit to run these," Jack said. "And even more checks before we actually get started. Transfusing the wrong type is a disaster we don't want. Oh, I'll be back with coffee as soon as I can."

Jack was good to his word. He kept the coffee flowing and kept a close watch on Goode while Ed and Jazz found something to eat. An hour or so before dawn, a different nurse arrived bearing a plastic bag of blood.

"Where's Jack?" Landry asked.

"Taking a break," she said. "He asked me to get the transfusion started for him."

She busied herself hanging the bag of blood on the pole and connecting it to the fluid already running into Goode. Once she had it flowing, she left the room.

Landry and Jazz settled in to wait. Moments later, Goode groaned and began to massage his left side.

"Are you okay?" Jazz asked rising and going to his side. "My God, Landry, he's burning up. Call Jack."

Landry hit the nurse call button and stuck his head out into the hall. "We need help in here!" he yelled and remembered the word he wanted. "Stat!"

"What happened to all the checks Jack said would happen?" Jazz asked Landry.

"Goode, you're an ex-GI. What's your blood type?" Landry asked.

"B positive, why?"

"Cause that bag says A positive," Jazz replied.

Landry didn't wait, he pulled the IV from Goode's arm as Jack came through the curtain. Blood spilled onto the floor from the tubing. Landry clamped his hand over the bleeding IV site.

"Holy shit, who put this blood up there?" Jack asked.

He closed a clamp to stop the blood from leaking onto the floor. Looked at the bag and then at the band on Goode's arm.

"A female nurse. She said you were on break," Jazz said.

Goode's eyes rolled back, he went limp, and the machine attached to his arm began to scream. Jack punched a button on the wall above Goode's head. He hit another button, and the head of bed abruptly dropped. Jack threw the blankets off the bed. Doctors and nurses poured into the room, pushing Landry and Jazz out.

"Code Blue ER. Code Blue ER. Code Blue ER," blared overhead.

Landry lost track of all the people rushing in and out of Goode's room. Then, the rush suddenly stopped. Jack and a doctor came out and the news was written on their faces.

"I'm sorry," the doctor said. "Your friend didn't make it."

CHAPTER 29

Landry and Jazz dragged themselves through Sam's door and dropped down on his sofa. Sam made his way from the kitchen and looked them over.

"You look like cr—you look horrible," he said.

"Rev. Goode is dead," Landry announced, his voice flat.

"What? How? What happened?"

"They called it an acute hemolytic reaction to the blood he received," Jazz told him. "But it was murder."

"Murder, how?"

"He was given the wrong blood on purpose," she explained. "The police are still questioning the hospital staff looking for the nurse who did it."

"We don't think they'll find her," Landry added. "Goode told us a witch was in his room earlier. That's why he left the hospital. We failed him."

"He needed blood," Sam said. "How were you to know?"

"We should have been suspicious of a new nurse," Jazz said.

"Pardon me, but that's nonsense," Sam said. "You were exhausted. No one could fault you if you had come here and gone to bed. You went the extra mile for a friend."

"Maybe," Landry said. "But it still feels like failure to me."

"I may have a solution," Sam told him. "Confession is good for the soul. The new priest will be arriving this morning. I'm calling it a sign from heaven. Still, I'd like you to accompany him into his new office."

"Can you keep him out for a couple of hours? I need to close my eyes," Jazz said.

"Done," Sam said. "He's supposed to arrive at noon. Kevin and I will arrange to take him to lunch before he sees the church."

"Okay, but be careful. Trust no one, not today," Landry said.

"I will," Sam replied. "Coffee?"

"Beer," Landry and Jazz answered as one.

"Aw, one more hour," Jazz moaned.

"We have to get to the church," Landry told her. "I want to go in that office first."

"Must you always be so gung-ho?"

"Always, now get up.'

"I must have a shower before I leave this house," Jazz said, climbing out of bed. "Did you sleep at all?"

"Of course."

"Closing your eyes for fifteen minutes doesn't count," she said over her shoulder on the way to the bathroom.

"It was an hour," he said under his breath to the closed door.

Despite Landry's pacing and fretting about time, they reached the church ahead of the deacons. He hurried Jazz inside and down the hall to the priest's office. He took the knob in his hand, paused to look at her, and sighed.

"Into the valley of death rode the six hundred," he said and opened the door.

The volley and thunder that Landry half expected didn't happen. He escorted Jazz to a seat at the desk and sat down beside her. They sat in undisturbed silence until Jazz finally looked at her watch.

"Let's go meet the new priest," she said with a smile.

Sam was busy making coffee when they entered the deacon's office. He poured them each a cup and carried the cups over to Landry and Jazz.

"Where's the priest?" Landry asked.

"Kevin is showing him the nave and trying to explain the police tape. I saw your, or should I say, my car, didn't find you here and knew where you were."

Jazz nudged Landry in the ribs.

"And your findings?" Sam asked.

"We weren't in there that long," Jazz said. "And a surprise for the new priest is not out of the question."

"Shall we join them?" Sam suggested.

Leaving their cups behind, Landry and Jazz followed the deacon into the church.

"Father Michael," Kevin said. "This is Mr. and Mrs. Landry. They are visiting from New Orleans."

"New Orleans. From the city of voodoo to the city of witchcraft, are you the sort who are fascinated by the supernatural?"

"It does seem to come up wherever we go," Jazz answered. "My husband seems to find the subject rather tedious."

"I agree, Mr. Landry. All the superstitious hocus pocus gets tiring quickly."

"It really does wear on a person," Landry agreed. "We were acquaintances of Father Paul and hoped to see where he lived and worked.

"I was just on my way to see my office. Perhaps you'd like to come along. If you don't mind, Kevin."

"Not at all. Right this way."

"Wonderful," Father Michael pronounced his new office. "I simply love the bookshelves. I'm going to be very happy here."

"The shelves *are* amazing," Jazz said.

"And all the books. I see several excellent titles here. I don't see Father Paul's book though."

"I'm afraid it was stolen. Probably during the break in," Sam said.

"Just as well," Father Michael replied. "Paul was a good man, but his wild ideas about witches and witchcraft completely ignore modern science and reasoned thinking. He was so rational and insightful when it came to everything else."

"This entire city seems to refute that notion," Landry said. "Thank you, deacon, for showing it to us."

"I think we should be going now, dear," Jazz told him. "We have taken up enough of the deacon's time. And we still need to pack before our flight this evening."

"Let me show you out," Sam offered.

When they were outside, Sam turned to them. Landry held out his hand to the deacon.

"I think your office problem is solved," Landry said, shaking hands. "Father Michael is not likely to cause waves or stir up opposition. Things should quiet down now."

"But it's not solved," Sam said.

"It's never going to be 'solved', it's like world peace," Jazz said. "It can't be had until you reach the final chapter of *your* book."

"Meanwhile an uneasy truce is the best we can hope for," Landry added. "You have that."

"And we have babies to get back to," Jazz said.

"Of course, I understand. But no handshake for you." Sam embraced her. "Thank you. Thank you both."

They called a taxi to take them to the airport and the flight Clara had arranged for them that morning. They checked their bags at the curb and went inside. At check in, Jazz tapped Landry on the shoulder.

"What is it?" he asked.

"Put the boarding passes in your pocket and step over there with me."

"Okay," he said. "Now wh—oh, okay. How nice, we have someone to see us off.

Landry and Jazz gave the terminal a good-bye wave and headed for their gate.

ABOUT THE AUTHOR

Vietnam veteran, ordained minister, registered nurse, and vagabond tilter at windmills. Jack LaFountain is the author of 20 books, including the Mann of God books and his Red River series. Witch Moon marks his return to the Ed Landry "Moon" series after publishing his first fantasy novel. Jack makes his home in Harvest, Alabama.

www.jacklafountainauthor.com
www.facebook.com/authorjacklafountain
www.houseofhonorbooks.com
www.facebook.com/houseofhonorbooks

Be sure to sign up for the House of Honor monthly newsletter to keep up with all our latest releases.

PRAISE FOR THE AUTHOR

Krampusnacht
Karen Boyett

5.0 out of 5 stars **Very good!!**
Reviewed in the United States on February 25, 2024
I thoroughly enjoyed these stories!! Mr. LaFountain is a wonderful author!

Wolf Moon
Vivian Hearne

5.0 out of 5 stars **Aaaghhh!**
Reviewed in the United States on May 20, 2023
Verified Purchase
That was fun! Excellent Ed Landry novel! I hate cliff hangers! Please tell me the next one is out soon!!!

Blood Moon
Steve M.

5.0 out of 5 stars **A genuine good old fashioned scare!**
Reviewed in the United States on February 9, 2022
Verified Purchase

If you're looking for a romance novel with sexy monsters, DO NOT read this book. LaFountain has restored my faith in the genre of true horror novels. Although both novels are quick reads, they lack nothing in character development, plot twists and turns and good old fashioned scary as hell monsters. Loved both novels and look forward to Ed Landry's next encounter! Please don't keep me waiting Jack!

BOOKS BY THE AUTHOR

Ed Landry Novels
Bayou Moon
Blood Moon
Voodoo Moon
Lover's Moon
Wolf Moon
Hunter's Moon
Witch Moon

Red River Series
Death Rides the Red River
Death Haunts the Red River
Death Stalks the Red River

Short Story Collections
Tracks
Tokens of Perdition
Krampusnacht:
An Ed Landry Christmas and Other Stories
Dead Man's Hand
Dead in Deadwood

Mann of God
Redemption
Judgment
Zion
Resurrection

Experimental Christianity

Trails of Trouble

Coming Soon
Roads of Battle
the sequel to Trails of Trouble

Made in the USA
Columbia, SC
06 March 2025

54737104R00100